IRRESISTTBLY WRONG

Jennifer Remidas

CONTENTS

CHAPTER 1

I had been told, by philosophers and misfits alike, that high school would either be the best thing that ever happened to me or the worst. It was a dangerous time, they claimed: a time of uncertainty, of confusion, and if you were lucky, of love. As I sat idly on a bench on the outskirts of campus with droplets of rain harshly brushing against the umbrella above me, I knew that my experience would be anything but great.

With the exception of the gloomy weather, the day had been fairly lively. Nevertheless, it had been an urgent feminine squeal that had disrupted the equilibrium that evening. "God!"

One word, a simple breath: it echoed across our campus, breaking the ordeal stillness. Given the girl's panicked, frenzied state, I had thought that something drastic had happened to her, like perhaps her family had been washed away by the typhoon in the Philippines last week. If not affliction due to a natural catastrophe, then at least something drastic of the sort.

After she inadvertently gathered the attention of everyone there, she shouted to her friend: "Valerie, my septum! It's been fucking enlarged by the goddamn surgery!"

I blinked, biting my tongue to suppress my laughter.

"Calm the fuck down, Allen," was the response she had gotten.

People are stupid, my best friend, Joey, would often say. I would tell her that optimism was all that we had—because it was. However, then and there, bound to that social atmosphere, my faith in humanity began to deplete. Girls in our boarding school, Victorian High, had the habit of making drizzles sound like downpours.

I looked above the book I was reading, a classic by Kundera himself, only to be greeted by two pairs of unfamiliar faces. I wondered how the two girls could be preoccupied with something so infinitesimal when the world was plummeting into all of us. When living in a time of polarity and controversy, how was it that they were talking about this? Oblivious to the downpour, they bickered about the size of each other's noses as if their lives depended on it.

I tried to ignore them...I really did. However, trying to avoid conflict in situations like these never worked out, given that the voices of these two royalties were more irritating than Dolores Umbridge and Bellatrix Lestrange combined.

It took less than a second for me to slam my cover of The Unbearable Lightness of Being roughly on the table. A glare eminent on my face, I stormed over to where they were: just a table away. "Can you two not?" I demanded, scowling. It might have been socially suicidal of me to purposely get on their bad sides, but the way they talked made me want to yank out the hair on their heads and feed it to the Evil Witch of the West.

"Excuse me?" the first of the two said, eyeing me in disbelief. She snapped her bubblegum and raised her neatly plucked eyebrows.

"Can you two please lower it?" I asked, making an attempt to seem polite. "I'm kind of trying to read here," I picked up my book and shook it, "and you're disturbing the vibe."

"Yeah, whatever," the other one muttered, dismissing me with a wave. She flipped her hair in dismissal before resuming the conversation she was having with her friend, ignoring my protests altogether. Shaking my head, I picked up my copy of the novel on the table and marched towards the entrance of the campus, finding the scent of books growing heavier with every step.

Saying that our campus was beautiful would be an understatement. Grand, exquisite, breathtaking were all more appropriate terms.

My tattered pair of Oxfords squeaked as they made themselves across the muddy path to the entrance. As I entered the building, a familiar cacophony reached my ears: footsteps pounding up and down the hallways, rustling paper, slamming lockers and eager chatter.

As I wearily made my way towards my dormitory, a vivid frown still plastered on my face, my body abruptly collided with a figure akin a pole. Immediately, I stumbled backwards, my feet threatening to lose their security.

Inwardly groaning for not having been aware of my surroundings, I fixed my posture. It was only then that I realized that it wasn't a pole that I had bumped into, but an actual, living, breathing human being. When I finally found the right words to say, I spoke up with more venom than I thought myself capable of: "Watch where you're going next time." I was still aggravated from the encounter with the girls; I was not the brightest person to bump into that afternoon.

I heard a gentle hum leave the stranger's lips.

It was only when I raised my eyes to get a good view of him that I realized how attractive he was. He had short, messy hair that fell short of his eyes, and complementing grey eyes and pale skin.

His face is familiar, I found myself thinking.

Without a word, he left, leaving me alone in the corridor without having muttered even a simple apology. And that was all it took; that was how it began.

CHAPTER 2

Is it possible to dislike a boy you have never second glanced?

Joey, my best friend, didn't agree me when I told her that it was.

"Absolutely not," she said, rolling her eyes at me for even suggesting the idea.

It was nearly eight o' clock and we were both in my dorm room, anxiously cramming on our last minute homework that consisted of annotating Shakespeare's play, Hamlet. I bit my tongue as I glanced at an advertisement that was plastered on a billboard somewhere in the distance, one that was suggesting physical ther-apy for accident rehabilitation.

"Seriously?" I asked Joey, pressing my lips to-gether. Given that I had filled her in on every-thing that had happened yesterday, starting from when I had encountered the two preppy girls outside of campus, to the part when I had crashed into that stranger in the hallway, her reaction shocked me.

"Of course," she replied. Joey was adamant on finishing her annotations on the Shakespearean play, so she dismissed me with a wave before continuing to scribble with her pencil. "You can't like or dislike someone by just looking at them once. And you were just moody because of those girls, Avery. Don't jump to conclusions, okay?"

"Ever heard of first impressions?" I retorted, looking away from her.

I stared around my room, my mind in a haze.

Despite the grand size of campus, the dorm rooms were forcefully wedged between two other tightly compact rooms. My dorm, which I shared with one other girl: Molly, was composed of wooden floors and red walls, which were mostly covered with rock posters and graphic vinyl designs. The radiator had been doodled on with dark Sharpie markers, its edges designed with lyrics, lines of poetry, doodles and inspiring quotes.

"But tell me," Joey finally said, the corners of her lips twitching into a smirk. She dropped her pencil on her binder and momentarily began to massage her fingers. "On a scale of one two ten, how hot was he?"

I laughed, muttering a quick "eight" before shooting her an amused glance.

Joey squealed and before I knew it, her eyes were plastered on me, that senile smirk still plastered on her face. "You know that that means, right?" she asked me, raising both of her eyebrows in anticipation.

"Joey."

She nodded.

"Joey, there are over a thousand kids in this school. No way could that have been him."

News had gone around that there would be a new kid—a boy—arriving in our grade sometime soon. All of the girls had gushed over the possibility of him being a foreign exchange student, despite the teachers having announced that he was moving over from Michigan.

Joey smiled her contagious smile, passing it down to me. "It's like the movies," she said, grinning. "You bump into a guy. Your eyes meet and instantly, there's that brilliant connection. Then, the two of you fall in love and spend nights dreamily staring—"

I didn't want to dampen the mood, but I hadn't felt an instant connection.

Ignoring Joey's blissful trance, I took out my history textbook and sat on my bed quietly, contemplating whether or not I should head to tutoring. The first class of the day was instructional support—a free period, in other words—and the only way I was ever going to get my homework done was by forcing myself into a classroom.

"You've been reading too many romance novels," I muttered under my breath, sighing as Joey continued to trail off. "You know what, Joey," I finally said, interrupting her. Shoving my textbooks into my backpack, I gave my best friend a look. "I'm going to head to Ms. Watson's room for a little extra help in history."

Joey groaned, finally dropping the subject of my love life, or lack thereof. "History," she mumbled, sighing. "Thanks for the reminder that I'm failing that class."

I dismissed her by shoving my papers on my backpack. "Be sure to lock the door and leave the keys under the mat," I reminded her. Once she provided a swift nod of the head, I walked out of my room and headed towards the history classroom on the other side of campus.

Once I reached, I found that instead of our regular usual Ms. Watson being behind her desk, a handsome young man, probably in his early twenties, occupied her spot. His figure was tall and built, and enhanced by his navy blue suit and red tie.

I sat down on the chair nearest to whom I believed was our substitute for the day. "Hello, I'm Mr. Anderson," the stranger introduced tersely, as if he had been practicing all morning. "Are you here for tutoring?"

The room was empty, bereft of any presence except mine.

"I'm just here to study," I answered with a subtle smile.

"Let me know if you need any help," he replied, folding his arms across his chest.

I nodded.

Everything else that happened in that history room was completely unanticipated. A strange set of events had unfolded that morning, all of which oddly caught me by surprise. It wasn't that I had fallen madly in love with my new history teacher or anything, nor had I gotten involved in an intimate conversation with him regarding our futures, like they do in romance novels.

Actually, I had been doing the contrary: reluctantly answering questions about the Neolithic

Revolution. It was then that the boy that I had crashed into yesterday came marching in. The teacher, Mr. Anderson, greeted him the same way he had greeted me, before flipping to the next page of the novel he was reading, which was The Kite Runner by Khaled Hosseini.

The brooding boy took the seat next to me, and my breath hitched in my throat.

In the short time that we endured one another, neither of us uttered a single word. He was good at maintaining silence. Yet he preserved unnerving eye contact. I found that he would glance at me when he thought I could not see him, but my vision had no peripheries and his grey eyes were impossible to overlook.

And that was precisely how instructional support had gone by: with Declan Andrews—I assumed this was his name because it was what he had written atop his paper—sitting next to me, and our arms nonchalantly caressing once every blue moon.

CHAPTER 3

BEFORE He left us, my father would say that art feeds the senses of the soul. He was an artist not only in his profession, but in heart; he was a visionary. He enjoyed telling me that I had the potential to create magic with a simple brushstroke. To his satisfaction, I enjoyed painting; I enjoyed it so much that I spent hours building the perfect shade, and even longer creating concise portraits. His constant reminders that creation would expose me to a beauty beyond human capability did wonders to my artistic capability.

Needless to say, I was a little too ecstatic to be in art class that morning.

"Partnerships," Mr. Camia, our art teacher, began. "Everyone will be working with a partner for this one month project."

The boredom that had been pervading the air of that messy classroom dissipated into excitement. It was a mutual understanding between students and teachers that a partners-project was a ticket to wasting away the entire unit. I, however, was ready to create.

"But," Mr. Camia continued, garnering the attention of every student in the classroom. "I'll be the one doing the assigning." The entire class groaned in unison. "Think of it as an opportunity to get to know a person you normally wouldn't." Then ignoring our silent pleas, he began reciting partnerships. I contemplated asking him if I could work alone. I was never much of an extrovert, especially when it came to a subject as vulnerable as this one.

I exposed myself through my pieces, and I was not ready to be intimate with another.

"Alex Martinez and Andrea Lopez," he started.

I crossed my fingers, hoping that I would at the very least be partnered with someone I got along with. There weren't a lot of people—with the exception of perhaps Joey and a one-time acquaintance, Allie—that I knew here. Given that I had the social enthusiasm of a hermit, to say that I was no longer looking forward to being here would be an understatement.

"Joey Taylor and Carson Dawson, you two will be partners. Lee Anderson and Andrew Kim, you two should come and see me tomorrow in tutoring. Alison Bradley and Finn Cooper."

When the seconds turned into minutes and Mr. Camia had at last finished assigning our partners, I wearily stared at him, wondering why he had not called my name. With a disappointed resolve, I walked to his desk. "Mr. Camia," I said sheepishly, fixating my gaze on his. "You didn't call my name."

He looked up from the stacks of heavy of papers lined on his desk, his gaze deflecting from my cowering figure to the hustling classroom.

"Was anyone else not called?" he called out, staring at the class expectantly.

A familiar voice rose from the back of the room. As my eyes wandered to the origin of the sound, my jaw dropped. My suspicions had been proven correct. Of course it was him: the infamous Declan Andrews in all of his glory. Was this fate? If it was, why did it feel so terse? More importantly, how the hell did I still remember his first and last name? Was that fate?

"Mr. Camia," Declan said, a small smirk etched onto his face. "I don't have a partner."

My face fell.

It was hard to tell why I was adamant on spending as little time with Declan as possible. Whether I admitted it or not, the idea of his presence put me on edge. I could not endure it for a minute, let alone an entire month. I had absolutely no reason to despise him in the way that I did, no reason to be so irked by his every action, but I did. I couldn't bring myself to trust him.

The more I rummaged my mind for an explanation as to why this was, the more clear it became that he was a triggering symbol for a person in my life I had long wanted to forget. Liam, I concluded; thoughts of my relationship with Liam, my first love, clouded my mind. Every time I stared at Declan, I saw the familiarity in their eyes, their lips, and hell—they even shared a similar jaw. Their resemblance was starkly uncanny.

"Alright," Mr. Camia said, scribbling something onto one of the papers in his pile. He looked up at the two of us—at me, who stood in front of him, and at Declan, who was feverishly sauntering toward me—and smiled. "Declan and Avery, you two are set for the next few weeks. And since Declan is new, Avery, why don't you give him a tour around the school after class?"

"Mr. Camia, I'm sure that won't be necessary," I blurted out.

"I'm sure that's not true," Mr. Camia replied obliviously. "What do you think, Declan?"

My gaze traveled to Declan, who still had a provocative smirk plastered on his face. "I'd love for her to give me a tour," he said calmly, allowing his smirk to morph into a smile. It would be the first time I saw him smile; I saw Liam's smile from years ago.

"It's settled then!" Mr. Camia finalized, shooing us away. "Good luck, you two."

"I can't wait," Declan added, only for me to hear.

Groaning inwardly, I ambled towards one of the empty tables in the studio room, marking it as my territory before anyone else had the opportunity to do so. Declan caught up with me not much later, occupying the empty space beside me before I had the chance to object.

Not much after we got seated, he began digging his backpack for supplies. I sat on my desk, examining him out of curiosity. A conspicuous scar stood beside his left eye. Despite my unfair and inexpiable resentment for this boy, I had to resist my urge to lean across the table and run my fingers across it. I would if it was Liam.

I looked away.

When I heard shuffling, the signal that he had begun working, I sighed. "Hey, Declan, what do you want me to do?" I asked politely. His concentration was unyielding. He ignored me, and I pressed: "Declan?"

He leaned back against his chair. "Oh, so you're talking to me now?"

I looked at him, taken aback. "What are you going on about?"

"Ever since I got here, you've been nothing but cold. Avery Wilson, is it?"

I looked away from him, my heart sinking. "Of course. Listen, about that, I'm sorry."

"Whatever," he answered flippantly.

Just like that, I was back to despising Declan all over again. This time, it had very little to do with Liam and entirely to do with the fact that perhaps this boy was not all others pegged him to be.

In frustration, I placed my hands on the table. My clumsy movement led to my accidentally bumping onto the cold water glass placed next to Declan's canvas. Before I could atone it, it dawned on me that I had dropped below freezing water all over Declan and his art piece, causing not only his pants, but also his painting to change color in dampness.

The dropping of the glass on wooden tiles caught Mr. Camia's attention. He stared at us with arched eyebrows. "Is everything okay?" he questioned insipidly, staring at us with a gaze void of enthusiasm. He was a dull man who did not want to address us if he did not have to.

"Everything's fine!" I assured, furiously nodding my head.

Though unconvinced, he tore his gaze away from the two of us. As he resumed working on his desk, I haphazardly sauntered towards the napkin cabinet in order to grab a few for the wet floor and Declan. When I returned, I saw that his cheeks were tinted with a natural scarlet.

I stifled my laughter as I leaned toward the floor to clean the mess.

Declan Andrews took my bending down as an opportunity to grab my waist.

"You're such an annoying little piece of shit," I blurted out, slapping his hand away. I threw the wet napkin, knowing that they had been infected with the germs on the floor, at Declan. His reflexes patted it away effortlessly. "Leave me alone, Declan," I demanded, pouting my lips.

"Come on, Avery Wilson," he began with a low chuckle. "I hope you know by now that love and war both begin with a simple word."

I furrowed my eyebrows in confusion. "What the hell does that have to do with anything?"

My uncertainty seemed to amuse him.

"You know what," I continued. "I'm just going to ignore you. Bah. Pretend you don't exist." And that was precisely what I did: I worked on our assignment from afar, brainstorming possible topics, and eventually drove myself to ignorance of the knowledge of Declan's existence. When the bell rang at last, it was he who approached me with no signs of caution.

"The tour," he began. "Remember?"

I bit my lip harshly in dismay.

CHAPTER 4

"YOU know it's not going to work out if you keep acting this way, right?" Declan muttered, trailing behind me. I was giving him his tour with bitter apathy. I could barely look at him as we breezed through the corridors; I could understand if it was mutual and that he never wanted to see me again.

Pointing towards the cafeteria, I spoke up. "That is the cafeteria. We like to call it the cafe. You go in there every fifth period. It, obviously, has benches, and you eat food there."

Declan provided an incredulous glance. "You're seriously doing this," he deadpanned.

Ignoring him, I walked towards the auditorium, reactivating my robotic voice. "That is the auditorium. You sit there in assemblies. Sometimes you watch movies in there, give speeches, or if the principal has something important to say, he'll invite everyone in there."

"Just take me to English, Ave," he said with a sigh. "That's probably way better than this."

I released a sigh of relief. Then I escorted him to this class that we both shared. Ms. Jensen, our teacher, acknowledged us with a smile. "Ooh, and who is this?"

"New kid," I provided vaguely.

Ms. Jensen chuckled as I brushed past her on the brisk journey to my desk. "Why don't you introduce yourself...Declan?" she suggested, glancing at the attendance sheet atop her clipboard.

He nodded, accepting his several minutes of fame. This is it, I thought. This was the time for him to reveal everything that he wanted us to know about him. This was what he would expose about himself in a room full of strangers. Then the disappointment came:

"Hello. I'm Declan Andrews, and I believe that people are conquests," he began, then his eyes briefly met mine. "I suffer from boredom and the belief that human beings are mediocre as hell. Maybe that explains why I got expelled from my last school for placing a guy in a coma."

I released a startled gasp.

Declan chuckled, rolling his eyes. "Can't take a joke?" he retorted, but his eyes were on me, laced with a telepathic challenge.

Mrs. Jensen let out a nervous chuckle. "Okay then. Off to your seat, darling!"

The class then passed by in a blur. For the remainder of the day, I heard small-talk in hallways and in locker rooms about a new boy who had the eyes of ice. There was the occasional, "Shit, the new kid is like totally hot!" and the "I'd fuck him hard" from the girls in cheerleading.

If fate was hearing his name everywhere I went, I had fallen a victim to destiny.

CHAPTER 5

MY father left my mother because she was naive. When he was in rehabilitation for his alcoholism, she found uncoordinated solace in the arms of another man. It was the right kind of wrong, she would justify; I had not forgiven her since. It was not just for cheating but because she forced the only man I ever loved out of my life. Papa was a precious token of my childhood, and I despised my mother for driving him away.

"And that is why I don't want to come home for Christmas, Mom," I clarified onto the other end of the line. "You asked me why. There. You have your answer." Talking to my mother always unleashed the worst in me. By the end of every session, I was a breathless, incoherent mess.

My mother had begun placing me in boarding school at the age of seven. It was to fulfill her dreams of fame and glory. At thirty two, she had achieved it at last through a movie role in one of Hollywood's top rated films, but it had come at the expense of everything we could have had. Your father chained me, she would say. I sacrificed my life to be his caretaker. Was it too much to ask her to do the same for me?

"But, Avery, honey..."

"But nothing, Mom. I'm not coming."

"Mark insists," she implored. "He really wants to meet—"

I cut her off by ending the call. It was the same routine: ardent phone calls during which she begged me to live with her and Mark, her husband and the man that had taken Dad's place in her life. I scoffed in frustration.

It was then that the door to my dormitory flung open, revealing an excited Molly. She was my roommate and from the beam on her face, I predicted trouble. Without sparing her a second glance, I bolted to my bed, covering my face within a sanctum of comforters.

"Oh, stop it Avery! I'm not going to force you to go to a bar with me again!"

I said nothing and let silence ensue.

"But remember? You got wasted that time around and I gave you a ride. You said you owed me. Owe it to me now because I have the best idea!"

I resisted a cough itching on the base of my throat. Nothing good could come out of any of Molly's many infamous ideas.

"There's a party going on tonight. You have to come with me."

Here was a thing about Molly: whenever she used obligatory words such as "have," she meant it. She meant it even if it meant putting you on a leash and dragging you there. Of course, I was stubborn too. "I'm not going," I stated solemnly.

"Yes, you are."

"No I'm not."

"Yes, you, like, totally, are!"

I released a sigh. "Um, no, I, like, am totally not."

"Don't mock me, Avery," she chastised. "You're going and that's it. Dot. Period. Finale. Anyway, Joey's going too! That should be motivational factor uno."

I laughed. "And just because Joey goes I should go?"

"Yes, Avery, just because Joey goes, you should go."

"Parties are bad," I reasoned.

"But they're fun!"

I scrunched my nose. "Hormonal teenage boys."

"Vodka," she sang.

"Sweat," I retorted.

"Free food!"

I pouted, giving in at last. "Maybe, if there's free food."

"There's Japanese," she clarified. "It's going to be in that nice restaurant that just opened."

"The one with spicy tuna sushi and a sushi burrito?"

She nodded, a devious smile overtaking her face. "So you're coming."

I looked away.

She squealed, jumping up and down in excitement. "You won't regret it, Avery," she assured. "I promise."

CHAPTER 6

THE first thing I saw upon entering the restaurant was a string of flashing neon lights. Then everything else followed: the hormonal boys and sweaty teenagers, as I had anticipated, and Molly's promise of plates upon plates of delectable Japanese cuisine and a seemingly unending abundance of vodka. It made the prospect of sneaking out and facing possible expulsion if we were caught a little more tolerable.

As Molly, Joey and I stepped inside the platform of the party, the music intensified. I felt feverish, like the drumming was in accordance with my heartbeat. Whenever the beat dropped, so did my heart to my dismay.

I was beginning to enjoy the scenery when a guy bumped into me in a drunken stupor, spilling his drink over my dress. I yelped as he mumbled an incoherent "Sorry" before breezing through the crowd.

Resisting a sigh, I gripped my wet dress. Molly offered a sympathetic look while Joey laughed. "Of course some nut would crash into you," she commented. "You're like the fucking epitome of a klutz, Avery."

I glowered at her, not yet having developed the ability to laugh at myself. "Whatever, Joe."

"Don't call me Joe," she retorted.

"Joe," I repeated, biting my lip.

"Ooh, look there!" Molly digressed, pointing towards the other end of the room. "Looks like the new kid if I'm not hallucinating again."

A wave of annoyance coursed through me.

It was Joey who dragged me over to where Declan was. Molly trailed behind us, enthusi-astic about a potential encounter with a boy who could mean absolutely everything to her but was beginning to serve as nothing but a nuisance to me.

"Declan," she began. "Hi."

I realized then that I wanted to be more like her: more enthusiastic to meet others and less dismissive of strangers that I knew virtually nothing about.

When I saw Declan's face behind the myriad of people in between us, I felt myself grimace. A combination of this chaotic atmosphere and the intoxication in the air did little to ease my hammering heart that craved to see Liam there instead of him.

"Hey beautiful," he said, winking at Molly.

From the corner of my eye, I saw a tint of scarlet coat Molly's cheeks.

"Guys, I'm going to get a drink," I said. The statement went ignored by Molly who was already submersing herself in Declan, and by Joey, who was now nowhere to be found. The song in the background became starkly illuminated in my journey to the bar.

What's somebody like you, doing in a place like this?

Did you come alone, or did you bring all your friends?

"...Say what's your name, what 'cha drinking, think I know what 'cha thinking..."

I snapped out of my mirage as that voice slurred the lyrics to the song.

"...I'll never be the same," he sang sporadically. "If we ever meet again. Won't let you get away, if we ever meet again..." He continued to sing, his eyes fixating on my stumbling figure. At first glance, my body gathered immeasurable warmth. As the stranger's familiar strands of blonde hair registered, and as I had the opportunity to fully outline his devilishly handsome features, it dawned on me that this boy was the long lost token of my past.

"Liam?" I questioned, leaning into him.

It was then that Declan came between the two of us. "Liam," he said. "There you are."

"Avery," Liam deadpanned, brushing Declan aide.

Declan's eyes deflected between the two of us. "You two know each other?"

"How do you know him?" I asked Declan, referring to Liam.

"He's my brother," he explained. Then he eyed me wearily. "How do you know him?"

"She's an old friend," Liam explained, biting his lower lip. With that gesture, our history could have been forgotten. And in the moment that he transfixed me with his gaze, I swore it was. "Nothing more than an old friend," he continued. "Right Avery?"

"Yeah, right," I answered nonchalantly, but all I could think in the back of my mind was that this explained everything between Declan and I. It explained our rotten start and the even more discouraging encounters that followed. It was because Declan physically embodied everything that I yearned to forget. He carried a part of Liam in his own presence, and Liam was cold: a heartbreaker even in his best days. We had been over before our relationship could breathe.

And here I was: stifling my relationship with Declan before our relationship could breathe.

CHAPTER 7

I was ruthless to a lot of people but I had even more of a reason to be this way around Liam. It was justified because he had torn me apart—completely dismantled my belief in love, what I had left of it anyway. Seeing him again, all I could remember was that night: the clouded, unclear night wherein I had caught him blind-sightedly with another woman. I hadn't even gotten the chance to see who she was.

"What are you doing here?" I questioned—sneered.

"I—"

"Wait," Declan interjected. "What I'm interested to know is how you two know each other."

"We used to be friends," Liam repeated. "I told you, Declan."

"Friends where? Friends how? Friends in what plane of existence?"

I bit my lip. "Tone it down a notch, Declan," I told him. "We were in boarding school together in secondary school. Liam was in with us." He was more than in, though. We had been intimate for almost a year. In hindsight, our relationship was nothing more than an intangible blur, a result of boredom at best, but I was convinced that I had been in love with him. And he had never thought to mention his brother?

Molly, beside me, shifted uncomfortably. She knew of my history with Liam; she had endured it with me. "William," she addressed with a hint of discomfort, annoyance, and perhaps intimacy.

I placed my hands on Declan's shoulder, leaning into his shaven cheeks that smelled freshly of lavender. "You know, Liam," I began, my voice just above a whisper. I let my tongue explore my lips, dampening them, and trailed my fingers across Declan's jaw. "You never told us you had such a hot brother."

Declan closed his eyes, devouring the touch, and a faint icon of jealousy crossed Liam's eyes as I kept my fingers on his brother's skin. Despite not having seen each other in what felt like eternity, the effect remained intact; we could unravel each other with a simple breath if we tried. Too bad I wanted to destroy him.

"So you know," he said.

"There's a lot that I know," I retorted. "But you've always known more, haven't you?"

Molly chuckled nervously. "Yeah, Liam. Shit. Why are you even back?"

"A circumstantial thing," he explained.

"Like what we had," I deadpanned. Because our love had been circumstantial too.

"What happened between you and Liam?" Declan questioned uncertainly. His eyes met mine once more, this time lacking the despondency that had accompanied his previous glances. Declan was softer—more inquisitive.

"Friendship. Romance. Sex. Whatever," I retorted, rolling my eyes.

"It's just that I don't fancy being a pawn in between whatever it is you two have left going on," he mumbled lowly enough for just me to hear.

"Love and war both begin with a simple word, wasn't it? It's beginning now, Declan. Because my word is revenge."

Declan chuckled in his silent amusement, and it was then that Joey approached us. "I came in the middle of something tense, didn't I?" she noted, catching onto the terseness in the air.

I pulled away from Declan. "Not at all."

"Just mending old ties," Liam said, leaning into her.

I took a step backwards from the four; I needed to leave.

"Where are you going?" I heard Declan shout as I began jostling towards the door.

"Don't follow me, Declan," I warned him, but who I was really warning was Liam. "I need air."

CHAPTER 8

"LAST night was wild," Joey beamed, sounding just like her regularly cheerful self.

"Yeah," I muttered. "Tell me about it."

Molly recoiled beside me. "Who would've thought he'd return?" she muttered. "Fucking Liam Andrews. I'll never forgive him on your behalf, Avery."

The three of us were seated in the cafeteria, discussing last night's events in detail.

"And we still need to discuss your behavior," Molly continued. "What was it with you suddenly becoming touchy-feely with Declan? Complete-ly inappropriate!"

"Shush it with the jealousy, Mols," Joey piped in. "We're discussing Avery's psychotic ex—not his slightly-more-tolerable brother."

I released a fleeting laugh. "Declan's not much better than his brother, honestly and objectively speaking. The Andrews are cursed."

"He's wise," Joey noted wistfully.

I shrugged. "So was Liam, once upon a blue moon."

"You know," Joey began, softening her glance. "Liam is a true bastard. What he did to you was really inappropriate. Who he did it with was even more inappropriate, and I cannot—"

"You know who he did it with?" Molly inter-jected, her eyes widening.

"No," Joey replied bluntly. Then she eyed Molly suspiciously: "Why?"

"So I could break her face, naturally," Molly replied curtly. "He destroyed Avery, didn't he?"

I swallowed.

He had. He had destroyed me in ways I had once believed unfathomable. Imagine a fourteen year old girl, one who believed in the picturesque fantasies of an epic true love, finding her boyfriend with another girl. Imagine the heartbreak that ensued, the chaos and the resentment, and the bizarre loss of self-esteem. It had been difficult, at times seemingly impossible, to continue about meeting other boys after Liam. I had been exposed to heartache a several years too early. Because here I was now, at sixteen, distrustful of everyone I met.

"When you left us last night, Avery," Joey began, "Liam told us something."

I looked between Joey and Molly expectantly, and Molly looked away.

"It's about him—this program transfer thing. He said he's going to be moving into our campus."

"And then I accused him of just antagonizing us," Molly said, "but he wasn't."

"Declan confirmed it," Joey added.

"And," Molly continued quietly, a frown materializing on her face. "I might have seen him dispatching his luggage from a car this morning."

I lowered my gaze in both disappointment and anger. "Well, shit."

For a moment, silence ensued.

"We all need a break," Molly muttered, releasing a lingering sigh. "We need to have a girls night out. First Declan and now Liam. It's getting suffocating, all of this excess drama. So we need a break. A spa day. A day out in the mall. An escape. Shopping!"

"Sounds necessary," Joey mumbled.

I caved in because I was too exhausted not to. "Yeah, that doesn't seem so bad right now," I told her, lifting my visage. "Thanks Mol."

She nodded slowly. "Of course. What are friends for?"

CHAPTER 9

"LOOK at this one! It's so fucking hot!" Joey exclaimed, beaming as she held up a skin-tight black dress.

"So buy it," Molly retorted, receiving a laugh from me.

It's hideous, I thought. I considered saying it aloud before hushing altogether.

"But I have no one to seduce," Joey muttered, placing it back on the rack. She picked it up again just seconds later, biting her lip. "Avery, you try it."

"I don't have anyone to seduce either," I stated monotonously.

"But it fits you! Like, your figure," Joey reasoned.

I gave the dress a once-over before dismissing it. "I'm not wearing that thing."

I ended up wearing it. My best friends were more stubborn than I was. They were pervasive of my desires and oddly successful at convincing me to do the very things that I vowed not to do. As I removed my clothes and slipped onto the dress, I slackened despite it clinging onto my skin.

"Hot as fuck," Joey commented when I walked out in uncertainty.

Molly agreed. "Buy that and seduce Liam," she encouraged tentatively, "and then when he's on the verge of cumming, leave him. Destroy that self-righteous bastard!"

I laughed, waving her off. "You're too much, Molly."

"Seriously, though," she pressed.

Dismissing her, I reentered the dressing room. It was then that the lights began flickering on and off. Grabbing my stack of clothes, I cleared my throat; it was precisely as I was preparing to remove the dress from my body that a pitch darkness overcame the room. In a frenzy, I sauntered out of the dressing room. I was unpleasantly surprised to find no one there.

Wondering where Molly and Joey had gone, I called out their names. Receiving no response, I followed the faint light trickling into the store from the front door to find my exit. I pondered the possibility of a gunman being in the mall; I could have been on the brink of death if I could not escape. I wondered if all of this was just a nightmare that I would awake from in due time.

As I stepped out of the store with a shoplifted dress clinging onto my body, I spotted Liam from the peripheries of my vision. He saw me too. I knew because he began approaching me, a taut boy trailing behind him. Razor, I came to know, was his name.

"You okay, Avery?" Liam asked me once mere inches deemed us apart.

I nodded, wanting nothing more than to brush past him into another existence. "Fine."

He took cautious steps toward me. "You look pale."

"I'm fine," I said snidely. "I need to get back to the campus."

"Me too."

"So I heard."

"Joey?"

I nodded. "Yeah. Joey."

"Sorry that you had to hear it from her," he said sincerely. I was almost fooled.

"You know, Liam," I began, my gestures a paroxysm of my pent-up resentment for him. "Standing in this forsaken mall lot and having a small-talk with you isn't really my idea of an ideal day off. So please, with your permission, may I leave?" I felt my jaw clench then.

He moved to the side apologetically, revealing a pathway to an escape. "But at least let me drop you off in campus," he offered. "I have a car."

"And I have public transport."

"Don't tell me you came alone," he murmured in—concern?

"I lost Joey and Molly in the blackout."

"So would it hurt you let me escort you? You don't even seem like you have a purse."

I looked down at my hands, where my clothes were. Of course I didn't have my purse; I had given it to Joey to hold while I was changing in the fitting room. Fuck.

"Um," I drawled sheepishly, swiveling on my heel. "On second thoughts..."

Chapter 10

IT rained on our short and unplanned journey to Liam's car. By the time we reached, Liam, Razor and I were drenched in rainwater. Liam had resorted to parallel parking because the mall charged money, and he (being a student) had little to spare. To my dismay, the storm increasingly gathered intensity and I had always been terribly afraid of thunder.

When lightning cackled in the distance, I had no option but to accept Liam's comfort. "It's okay, Avery," he would say. "Calm down. It's nothing. It won't hurt you." I was nostalgic for the days when I could accept those words without an ulterior thought barring my sense of peace.

"It's a good thing we spotted you, huh," Razor said softly.

I nodded. "Yeah, about that. Thanks bud."

Liam ruffled my hair. "Anything for you bud."

It was an additional ten minutes later that we reached Liam's car. He was an expert driver, breezing past the rain with an effortlessness that I had never stopped assigning to him. The roads were astonishingly clear for rush hour and the three of us talked about everything and nothing at all. I remember laughing and losing sense of myself and forgetting everything in the confines of that warm vehicle.

Liam stopped the car a several blocks away from campus. "Just so we don't get caught," he explained sheepishly; I nodded in understanding.

I waved goodbyes to both Liam and Razor before leaving the car. To my surprise, Liam began trailing behind me.

"Can I help you?" I asked him.

"Just wanted to drop you at the door," he said cheekily, and that was exactly what he did. When Liam left to find Razor, I entered the campus by hopping our fence. As I clumsily landed on the other side, I noticed a figure standing by the campus door. In fear that it was a watchman or worse: the principal, I cowered, lowering my head to avoid any gazes.

A little too late, I realized that the person on the other side was Declan.

"Fraternizing with my brother again?" he commented in bitter amusement.

"Not that it's any of you business, is it?" I retorted.

"You might want to watch your tone tonight," he cautioned.

"Why the hell would I do that, Declan?"

A corner of his lip twitched, foreshadowing a smirk. "Because I'm today's volunteer watchman."

My jaw dropped. "No."

"You overestimate me, Wilson," he said. "Give me one good reason I shouldn't rat you out."

"Because I'll have—uh—sex with you?" I offered, biting my lip.

He took a several steps closer, enclosing the proximity between us. "You do look good in that dress."

I looked away from him in disgust. "The fact that you responded that way says a whole fucking lot about your character," I blurted out. Then I chastised myself for being so impulsive.

He feigned a flinch, pretending to recoil. "Ouch."

I hardened my clutch on the clothes on my hands.

"But you look good, Avery," he murmured, softening his visage. "Pretty."

I scratched my head with my idle hand, gawking at him. "Seriously? I'm not even going to comment on your volatility, Andrews. You're insane."

He shrugged. "Yeah. Maybe. Still ratting you out though. Winning the genetic lottery doesn't guarantee you anything."

I felt an onrush of anxiety overcoming me.

"You wouldn't."

Would he?

CHAPTER 11

I took a deep breath, embracing myself for the worst. I can do it, I told myself in consolation; I can face expulsion. Did being expelled from Victorian High bar your entry into any other institution for higher education? Did it mean being an escort was a possibility in my foreseeable future? So many questions were invading my mind. Then there was Declan: oblivious to it all with his devilishly handsome features.

Winning the genetic lottery didn't guarantee him much with me either.

"The principal is in his office, expecting you," Declan said.

When I failed to react and simply remained glued onto the pavement, he released a sigh.

"What, Avery? Do you expect me to lead you there too?"

"Declan. Please mend this," I pleaded.

"The damage is already done," he murmured, vaguely pointing to the ceiling. When I followed his hands, I noticed that a video camera was parched atop us. Unsure of whether I should cry or scream, I growled. And when I did it again, Declan chuckled in his hushed, cryptic way.

"God, Wilson. Did you just growl?"

"I may cry," I muttered in dismay, clutching my wet clothes. In that moment, I was the epitome of pathetic and I wished that I could change into clean clothes before facing any ramification.

Declan suddenly burst out laughing. "Avery," he said. "Oh, Avery."

I pressed my lips in a thin line of indignation. "What?"

"I was only joking. I didn't rat you out—"

"And the camera?" I interjected.

"It doesn't work."

With that consolation, I leaned into him and harshly shoved him on the chest. "You dickhead," I muttered in rage. "What the hell is wrong with you? Why would you do that?"

He remained on position, unfazed by my assaults. I expected a snarky comment or even a physical retaliation—because this was Declan fucking Andrews and he had no reason to feel anything short of resentment for me—but he, releasing an exhausted sigh, took my wet clothes from my hands and took them into his own. "Let's clean you up?" he offered.

I blinked as a way to hold in my tears.

I led him to my dorm and felt the air growing increasingly terse with every step the two of us took forward. When inside, he racked my closet for a towel and gave it to me. I dried my hair and body; then it was time to change. "Are you going to stand here and watch me strip, Declan?" I commented sarcastically, but my heart was hammering sporadically by his mere presence.

His eyes widened. "I—uh—I'll leave," he said quickly.

"No, it's okay. I'll just go to the bathroom and do it."

He nodded. Then when I had changed and returned, he sat down on my bed with irises brimming inquisitively. "I wanted to ask out of curiosity," he murmured, scratching his ear. "What exactly happened between you and Liam?"

"Declan—"

"I get that it's bitter history," he added, "but much of Liam's life is a mystery to me. And you're in my life now. We have to do that stupid art project. And I don't know what that has to do with anything but just—please give me an answer. I don't expect one, but I was hoping for one."

"Why don't you expect an answer?" I asked him.

"Because it's none of my business," he responded curtly.

"Then why are you asking the question?" I pressed, purely to antagonize him.

He chuckled. "God, I knew you'd do this."

"What this?"

"That you'd stray from the topic with your sarcastic responses. It's what you do best."

"Well I'm sorry to say that whatever happened between your brother and I is none of your business," I snapped, rolling my eyes. "I owe you nothing, Declan."

"Alright, whatever," he retorted, standing up to leave. "So I guess the last few minutes never happened and that tomorrow we're just going to continue on as the strangers we are to one another. More banter. More meaningless arguments. Whatever satisfies you, Avery."

"Just leave," I muttered, saying not much else.

He stood up from my bed. "I guess I will."

"Bye."

"Yeah, whatever. Bye."

Chapter 12

"**B**LERG."

That was the first words to escape my lips upon seeing Liam walk past the school café, his eyes scavenging the unfamiliar territory for familiar faces. My first instinct was to walk up to him, to say hi, and to even insinuate a conversation, but then I realized that I never cared much for being a humanitarian.

I sipped my caramel latte because I was gone and Declan was the inexplicable culprit. Even with a glorious night's sleep and over twelve hours since our exchange, he was still fresh on my mind. I thought of him when I saw art; I thought of him when I saw brown-headed boys lacking direction; and I thought of him when I told myself not to think about him.

The fact that I had to return to Art class to finish this project with him was tormenting me.

"Avery!"

I choked on my latte. Then I saw Razor. "Oh, ha-ha," I heaved out. "Razor. Hi." Then behind him, I inevitably spotted Liam. "And Liam. You too. But have I mentioned that I'm actually out-of-bounds this morning? I don't want to see either of you right now, quite frankly."

Liam ignored me. "Hey, so where's room 307?"

"The seventh room on the third floor," I said incredulously. "Have you a brain?"

He rubbed his temples sheepishly. "Oh, right."

"Anyway, guys. I was being serious when I said that the morning is a time of solitude."

"It's nearly eleven," Razor said pointedly.

"Wait—" I blinked. "—what?" I checked my watch, which read half past seven. "Ha-ha. Good one, Razor," I complimented, wiping an imaginary tear from my eye. "Oh, that was good."

"Avery, your watch is wrong," Liam told me.

So I bolted to art. To Declan. "You're late," he commented snidely.

I occupied the empty seat next to him. "Sounds like you missed me."

"Only in your wildest daydreams."

"You don't want to know what happens in my wildest daydreams," I taunted.

He looked up at me. This is the point where I must refrain from speaking about his eyes, but his eyes. Was this what it was like to be en-tranced—to be entrapped—by another? "You're desirable," he stated. "If I dreamed about you at all, I would be fucking you in my wildest daydreams."

I rolled my eyes. "So. This project," I digressed. "Any ideas for the theme?"

"We should make a double perspective piece," he suggested shyly.

I leaned into him. "Yeah?"

"Like, on love—or something else. Whatever you prefer. You and I are complete opposites,

Avery, so I think it could work well. Like a Yin and Yang dynamic or something."

"I like it," I told him, nodding slowly.

"So what is it?" he asked me with anticipation.

I eyed him curiously. "What is what?"

"Your belief in love."

"It's a myth," I answered cynically.

He bit his lips as he savored my answer.

"I hate the human fascination with love," I continued. "All it does is result in heartache."

"My brother," he said then, "he spited you, didn't he? He gave you a reason to stop believing in love and everything associated with it."

"Something like that."

"Liam's a dick in that regard."

"And you? What does the famous Mr. Andrews have to say about love?"

A coy smile graced his face. "I guess you'll just have to wait and find out."

When art class—and a rather productive one at that—ended, Declan and I waved goodbyes in good terms for once in our lives. I was haphazardly shoving my books inside of my locker before my next class when Liam approached me.

"Not getting the hint, Liam?" I said to him.

He shook his head. "Don't tell me you don't believe in second chances."

"Not with you."

"So if I asked you to date me again right here and right now, you wouldn't consider it?"

I slammed the door shut. "No."

"Will you?" he asked me shyly. "Will you consider it?"

I narrowed my eyes at his face, at the way his eyes glistened with anticipation and his eyebrows that were scrunched in a gesture of sincerity. "I'm considering it," I told him. "Oh, I considered it. There. My answer is no."

He placed a hand on my cheek, making the area slacken with tingles.

"Liam," I chastised, slapping his hand away. "What is this?"

"My brother talks about you," he said cryptically. "It makes me nostalgic for you—for us."

"Oh, God," I muttered, rolling my eyes. I began the walk to my next class. "Leave me alone, Liam. First day back and you're already exposing your own shit."

"You'll consider it?" he pleaded.

I looked behind my shoulder. "Considering it. Considered. And the answer, once again, is no."

CHAPTER 13

B ECAUSE of the traffic in between classes and our own lives, I was only able to have a conversation with Joey a several days later. We met in my dorm room because it had become our unspoken sanctuary. When I told her about Liam, she lost her sense of peace. "He did what?!" she exclaimed, floundering for words and her sanity.

"I don't get him," I announced. "But yeah. Same dialogue, same expression. Verbatim."

"And, Avery, what exactly did you say?"

I shrugged innocently, pouting my lips. "Oh I don't know. What would you say if your ex-boyfriend cheated on you with an unknown girl and then he came back acting all sweet and lovable and asked you out in such a cute way that you seriously could not refuse?"

She gawked at me. "Yes..?"

I scoffed. "No."

She shrugged. "Good choice, I suppose, but a part of me wants you to break him, you know?"

"He's not a piece of glass," I told her. "He's made of steel."

"Liam fucking Andrews," she muttered in disapproval. "Has he approached you since?"

I shook my head. "I've been avoiding him like he's the plague."

"Funny you say that. Molly's been clinging to Declan like he's plague-medication."

I resisted the warmth that threatened to gather on my face. "Oh?"

Joey, noting the monotone in my response, eyed me cautiously. "You didn't laugh at my joke," she said pointedly. Then when I began to laugh tersely, she shrugged it off. "Anyway, they're supposed to be seeing each other right now or something."

"That's cool, I suppose," I said curtly.

My mind was racking up all the reasons that Declan would do this. Did he like her? Because fuck, I was concerned. I was just beginning to ponder the possibility that he might actually like me; and I may have considered a plane of existence wherein I felt the same way; and I may have even considered it happening within this plane.

And he was with Molly?

Of course he was—he had every right to be. He was in no way entitled to me, and he provided no sign that he even wanted to be. I told myself to calm down before doing just the opposite of that.

"Fuck," Joey cursed. "It's Liam—he's here."

I turned around to see that the door had been opened by the devil himself. "You're not invited here, Liam," I told him.

He rubbed his back sheepishly. "Sorry," he muttered before leaving without a word nor explanation as to what he was doing here. I dismissed it because it was the easier thing to do. And I was far more preoccupied with another Andrews—what was he doing with my best friend? Were they falling in love as Joey and I spoke?

"Oh my god! You guys will not believe what just happened to me!" Molly exclaimed, breaking through the door. Her dramatic entrance calmed my heart while simultaneously causing it to hammer sporadically.

"Molly," Joey began. "Are you not wearing...lip stick or lip gloss?"

"Shut up," she ordered, glaring at Joey.

I released a fleeting chuckle.

"Actually, Joey, I am wearing lipstick. It's just not dark. It's light."

"But that can't be it," Joey observed. "Why are you glowing, woman?"

Molly grinned. "So we were outside, right, sitting on the grass under a tree. He looked so cute today. And we were just talking about like, life, you know? Ah," Molly released a wistful sigh.

"It was after a little bit, but that was when he leaned in and kissed me."

"Um, who kissed you?" Joey asked.

Molly rolled her eyes. "Seriously guys?" she said incredulously. "Declan, of course!"

"Declan..?" Joey asked, causing me to gasp. "Declan kissed you..?"

My jaw clenched as Molly released yet another dreamy sigh. "Yes, Joey, yes," she exhaled. "Declan kissed me. And it was magical."

So it was. But then why was my heart being so reckless, acting as if Molly was undeserving of Declan's lips and that I was a better candidate? As Molly continued describing her evening in detail, I felt my heart fragmenting into tinier pieces. It was not that I was in love with Declan—it was too soon for that—but perhaps it was the truth that somewhere amidst this chaotic week of revelations and nostalgia, I had begun to rely on him for something beyond just a simple, innocent transaction? Maybe I relied on our fights and our blunt, profound encounters.

Snap out of it, Avery, my mind chastised.

I twirled my hair around my fingers, trying to hammer it home that Declan and I could never be anything more than a passing thought. But why was my heart telling pleading for otherwise?

Chapter 14

"IT was so dreamy. Like, my arms around his neck. Our lips meshing in what those cheesy romance writers call impeccable synchronicity. I sound whipped as hell but those bastards have it right. I have never experienced anything more beautiful..."

Molly was going on indefinitely about her kiss with Declan. So it was revolutionary. And it was doing more than just making her heart catapult; it was making mine wrongfully disintegrate. Why did I want Declan to leave Molly this instant and profess his affection or interest in me instead? Molly went around, I told myself;

she could find somebody else. By the end of my thoughts, I concluded that I was awful.

"Avery?" Joey mumbled, visibly troubled. "Is this what kissing Liam felt like?"

"No, Joey, this is not what kissing Liam felt like."

"Oh, hush it, you two," Molly demanded, glaring tepidly at the two of us. "You just don't know what it feels like to be in love."

I exchanged an incredulous glance with Joey. "Calm yourself, Juliet. You've only known the guy for a goddamn week," I blurted out. Then when Molly and Joey narrowed their eyes at me in astonishment, I brought my fingers to my lips. "Um, I mean, yes, love, whoorah?"

"Uh, okay, so Molly is in love," Joey digressed, eyeing me cautiously. "That's cool."

"Yeah. And dude. When you're in love," Molly began, tucking a strand of her hair behind her ear. Her eyes glistened with mirth. "Kissing your loved one feels like cotton candy."

"I'd rather it taste like vodka and sushi," I retorted.

The bell then rang, startling all three of us. Molly finally stopped prattling about her innocuous exchange with Declan. I wanted to tell her that it—love—was a mere illusion, and that this—whatever it was that she was feeling—was transient; it could not last; it could not be maintained, not even with the sincerest effort and integrity.

"Oh, well, earth to Avery!" Joey shouted. When I broke free from my trance, she added, "Time to go to class? Like, saved by the bell and all."

Molly rolled her eyes. "I'm just going to stay in."

"So bye," I said to Molly. Joey was kinder with her farewell. Then when we left the room and we were out in the wild, she slammed me against the wall and demanded answers.

"Don't tell me you've developed feelings for him, Avery," she stated.

I pushed her off. "I've developed feelings for nobody."

"So you're seriously telling me that you're in full approval of Molly's new relationship?"

"That's none of my business, Joey," I told her. "Why are you antagonizing me?"

"I'm not antagonizing you," she defended. "So you like him. And you feel attacked."

"I don't like him," I grumbled.

"Fuck."

I brought my hands to my temples, rubbing it. "Fuck indeed."

"You could've been a little quicker," Joey said.

"Quicker than Molly?" I retorted.

"Don't be a bitch."

"I'm not. Just—whatever," I muttered dismissively. "I have class."

Joey nodded. "See you then."

"Yeah," I said. "See you."

CHAPTER 15

JOEY and I ignored each other for days. Life was uneventful when I secluded myself from my best friends, so the weeks that followed unraveled uneventfully. Declan and I worked on our pieces individually. I worked feverishly on mine on the days I was free.

So far, I had painted an abstract piece that made me reminiscent of the days I had once been hopeful about love. Before the cynicism and before the distaste, I had believed in something extraordinary. I wanted nothing more than to revert to those days. It was easier to be happy when you were naive.

I sat on the stood behind my canvas, examining the piece. It showed the fragility of a woman who was slowly disintegrating like glass. I was satisfied with the result despite not yet being done.

I dropped my paint brush on the canvas edge, releasing a sigh. It was late afternoon and the campus was quiet. When I left my dorm and sauntered out into the courtyards, I came face-to-face with Joey. We glanced at each other for a moment, saying nothing. "I'm so sorry!" I said when, while she said, "We can't keep—"

A small smile materialized on my face. "You go."

"I was just saying that we can't keep going on like this, Ave," she implored. "I miss you."

"I miss you too."

"I knew you would."

I released a quiet laugh. "How's Molly?"

"I was just going to meet her, actually," she explained. "Come with?"

I agreed, and we talked amongst ourselves on the walk back into campus. Molly was in study hall jotting down notes. As Joey and I approached her, she acknowledged us from afar. We sat across from her before Joey broke the silence. "So?"

Molly bit her lip. "Hey."

"You're not in a good mood," I observed, glancing at her now glowering expression.

She softened her scowl. "It's just this assignment," she lamented. "I'm not even close to done and I have a date with Declan tomorrow night."

I smiled for her. "Hey, that's great. You two are getting pretty close, aren't you?"

"Yeah," she answered curtly. "It's nice."

Joey leaned in. "Hey, Mol, you okay? You're a little pale."

Molly plastered a smile that could have fooled us if we did not know her so well. "Everything is fine," she assured unconvincingly. Something was very clearly bothering her. It was then that I spotted a purplish mark faintly forming on her skin.

"Hey, is that a hickey?" I observed, raising an eyebrow.

Molly fixed her turtleneck to hide it. "Stop that, Avery."

"Declan?" I asked, suppressing the waves of emotions coursing through me.

She disgruntled, ambiguously nodding her head.

"Hot," Joey piped. She was smiling cheekily in happiness for Molly.

We indulged in the silence that followed in the next moments. It was Molly's voice that eventually broke it. "Hey Declan," she purred, glancing at a figure behind me. I felt his presence immediately, the shadow of his body descending before my own. He brushed over to the other side of the table, dropping an innocent kiss on Molly's forehead.

"Hey Mol."

She brought her fingers to his face squeamishly and Declan pulled away in a brash gesture laced with hesitance. Because I never pegged him to be a person afraid of public display of affection, I exchanged an incredulous glance with Joey. Something seemed wrong.

Something was certainly out of the ordinary if this boy was so visibly uncomfortable around my best friend who claimed to be crazy about him.

"Didn't know you'd be joining us, Declan," Joey said.

I contributed very little to the conversation as they began to banter. Then when Joey left and Molly claimed that she had to go run errands for community service, it was just Declan and I and a terse, unnerving silence that seemed to course in torrents between us.

"Do you mind?" he asked me once our eyes met.

I glanced at him questioningly. "Mind?"

"That I'm here," he clarified. "That I'm hooking up with your best friend."

"Hooking up," I repeated, stifling a scoff. "Quite the phrasing, Declan."

"I told you, don't you remember?" An indecipherable emotion crossed his eyes. "I believe people are conquests."

"Reevaluate that thought," I warned. "Because you break her, I swear to God I will break you."

He chuckled. "Gave her a promise ring last night."

"You've known her for less than a couple of weeks," I deadpanned, gaping at him. "How are you already making promises?"

He dismissed me with a flick of the wrist and coy words. "It was more of a symbolic gesture."

"Symbolic of what?" I asked in exasperation. "You've got the girl stuck in cloud nine when you clearly don't feel the same way. Are you even interested in her, Declan?"

He bit his lip in contemplation. It was then that he cleared his throat and said, "I'm interested in a certain someone that is cynical as fuck. Then again, she would be no more than a conquest either."

I burst then. "If you use the word conquest one more time, I swear to God—"

"I'm back!" a familiar figure announced. Joey. I released a sigh as she occupied the empty space next to Declan. "Seems like I walked in on an intimate conversation, again," she said with a laugh. "Why is it that I'm always coming into these situations?"

"Nothing like that," I told her.

I began undressing him in my head. Was it betrayal to Molly that I was emotionally, or even just physically, invested in him? Everything that I could have felt for Declan was no more than a bland, superficial affair. If anything, I was drawn to him for the mystery—for the promiscuity and the innuendos—and if I claimed to anything more, it would have been a lie. Was that treason in the handbook of maintaining friendships?

He put me on edge. On a verge. Of anger. Of desire. Of that dangerous feeling in between wherein your judgement is clouded by uncertainty. He made my thoughts appear in fragments. Everything felt disjointed.

"This is kind of awkward," Joey said tersely, her eyes deflecting between Declan and I.

I glanced downward at nothingness. Then Declan cleared his throat, suggesting that I look at him. When I did, he said with raised eyebrows:

"How about we go work on that art project now?" he asked me.

I raised an eyebrow in suspicion. "I thought it was a surprise."

"It is."

"Then it's a surprise, Declan," I deadpanned.

"Actually, I should be going, actually," Joey said with unease. She made her discomfort show.

"You just said actually twice," I told her pointedly.

She rolled her eyes. "Whatever. I'm off." Then she was gone.

"This is the part where I leave," I said to Declan, providing a brash glance in his direction. It was silent between us for a moment. And then he nodded, and that was my cue to get the hell out of there. And I did. But a part of me was counting down seconds until he called my name to stop me.

He never did.

CHAPTER 16

It was yet another infamous day in the life of Avery Wilson and I was headed straight for Art class—trouble, in order words; because Declan's presence was guaranteed.

Okay Avery. You must face him, I told myself. He didn't see you blow your snots or anything. You just know that he offered a promise ring from your best friend. Right now, just be calm, and pretend like nothing ever happened. Forget the fact that you're totally into him, and try not to remember the fact that he totally turns you on. Okay?

Did he ever feel for me too?

Ugh.

I entered the classroom silently. I had gotten some new colors for the painting aspect that we could have done in class. I refused to bring in my real piece until the day o our presentation; the paint Mr. Camia provided was limited, and we needed more color.

Speaking of color, where was Declan?

I quickly made my way towards our table, placing the paint on the desk as I sat down. My eyes wandered to Joey who was immersed in her project and a conversation with her partner.

I toyed with the colors to see what different combinations could produce as I awaited Declan's arrival. It was fourteen minutes into the class that a breathless figure arrived by the door; I had counted out of boredom. "Mr. Andrews," Mr. Camia addressed. "Would you please care you explain why you're—" He glanced at his watch. "—fourteen minutes late for class?"

"I'm sorry, sir," Declan said huskily. He carried the eyes of someone who had left his heart elsewhere. "It won't happen again."

"Too right it won't happen again. Now, please, go to your seat and help Miss. Wilson. Making her do all the work. Move along."

I felt my cheeks flush as Declan took the seat across from me, removing his bag from his shoulder. The frown that had plastered his face was replaced by a grin, however weak. "Making you do all the work? More like the total opposite," he said wearily, releasing a chuckle.

I laughed along and I wondered why. "I've been contributing," I said in my defense. "You just haven't seen it yet."

"How's that going?" he asked, seeming genuinely interested.

"Good."

"Do anything yet?"

"Actually," I drawled, biting my lip. "I'm almost done, Declan."

He let his shock show. "Really?"

I nodded. "Yeah, really. I like it—art."

"I've never been much of an artist," he stated softly. I wanted to tell him that he was—that despite his frequent remarks and sarcastic offerings, he spoke in ways that were memorable. He was an artist with his words, forming them with the expertise that made them cling onto your mind. He was an artist because he could make you feel insane with thoughts of him.

"But you are," I told him. "Your mind feels like an art piece, Declan."

He did not hide his shock as his eyes then met mine. "Really?"

I nodded again, this time in assurance. "Really."

It was funny that we were like this—that we could go from being utterly spiteful one moment to friendly in another. It was like we were two separate entities that converged once every blue moon, but that feeling of familiarity and bliss in that one fleeting experience was a reparation for any dismay the relationship had caused in the past.

Declan hesitated then again before he speaking up. "Avery?" he said, reluctance and caution etched onto his tone.

"Hmm?"

"Liam," he began solemnly. "He cheated on you, right?"

I felt my smile convulsing into an involuntary glower. I laughed in order to force back the tears that were already forming. I did not know why I felt like crying. Liam was over. He was the past. Here I was: I was my own present.

"You know, he really wants you back. He speaks of you."

"He was telling me that you spoke of me too," I said in an accusatory tone.

"Just spreading the worst gossip," he retorted lightly.

I laughed shortly. "Huh."

"Maybe you should talk to him though. Communication is key, you know. I hear him sometimes with Razor. He's always saying how much he misses you—"

"I thought you didn't believe in love, Declan," I interjected. "You're fooling me now."

He shook is head. "I don't. Maybe I do. I just—" He was interrupted by the shrill cacophony of the bell. He gave me a soft smile, ending his sentence without completing it.

"You just what?"

"Nothing," he replied.

I dropped the subject, letting the conversation dwindle.

We cleaned up quickly, placing the supplies and our projects—what we had of it—on the back sanctuary. Declan had a tendency to leave without goodbyes. When I slung my backpack over my shoulders and headed towards the door, he was already gone.

I sauntered towards the bathroom. Upon reaching, I stood before the mirror, listening to my sporadic breathing. A reflection of a frowning girl stared back at me. How could Liam still like her? She was no different than the others. She was cynical. She was untrusting. She was lonely—had a heart of stone. She'd had enough.

I washed my hands, fixed my makeup, and exited through the door to my locker. I had to stuff the notebooks that I no longer needed today into my locker. As I opened it, something dropped out, swirling in a blur of white onto the floor. I bended down and picked it up. It was a note. Poetry. It was from Liam.

Hey Avery. Declan helped me write it, but don't go falling for him, okay?

I read the poem with an open mind. It was certainly sincere and by the end of it, my heart was brimming with possibilities. I wanted nothing more than to forget these years that had come before wherein Liam and I were nothing. I wanted us to become something. But then I wondered how we could be anything after everything.

After the lies and after the torturous phase during which I had believed myself unworthy of anyone's love—how could I repeat it all over again? Because that was what forgiveness entailed. It meant I excused Liam's wrongdoings. It meant that I was giving him the possibility to do it all over again.

He ended the poem with a Meet me at the library after school. Please? —Liam.

I took in a deep breath and on my way to my next class, tossed the note into the garbage. I was already in so much trouble with Declan. I didn't want to be in even more trouble by getting involved with Liam. I would just get my heart broken. Again.

CHAPTER 17

"**Y**ou came."

I folded my arms across my chest, my eyes wandering to Liam's astonished ones. I know, I know. This was a mistake. That was just it; I was irrational. The more I thought about Liam, the easier it had been to latch onto our best days and ignore the worst. I wondered if he had truly changed and decided rather idiotically to take the risk.

"The poem was nice," I told him vaguely.

Liam leaned against the bookcases, his eyes not leaving mine. "I didn't think you would."

"But I did, Liam. So what do you want?"

"How have you been?"

A curt silence followed. I was at a loss of words because I hadn't rehearsed this. Every scenario that I had gone through in my head involved Liam going on with a speech, or begging for my forgiveness somehow. The vacant nature of the library added to our terseness. Time was suspended and it was just Liam and I—literally.

All I could think about was the fact that I had made out with Neil Armer behind these same bookcases just a year before. This space was tainted.

"I'm sorry I lied to you," Liam murmured, coursing his hands through his hair.

My eyes wandered to Liam's lips. "I still hate you with every fiber of my being."

"I know," he said. "Can I ever make it up to you?"

"I don't know, Liam," I told him truthfully. "You hurt me a lot."

"And you did too," he blurted out. Then he sheepishly glanced away, clarifying, "The poem. I found it in the trash. Spent a whole fucking week on that, you know? I didn't fancy it being surrounded by bubblegum and frozen tuna."

"So did you expect me to glue it to my wall?" I asked him incredulously. "Come on, Liam."

"It's just—"

"You should have saved a copy," I interjected.

He feigned a laugh. "I just expected a better reaction from you, that is all. And maybe I'm misguided. Maybe I'm not into you at all but still torn about the person you used to be," he speculated. I wondered if he knew that I was right there, then with his voice sharp: a mixture of hurt and anger. I avoided his gaze to see it again in my thoughts.

I sighed, relapsing. "Liam, it's just a damn poem."

"A poem I wrote, only for you. You know what, Avery. I'm tired of this. Of you running away."

I resisted an urge to roll my eyes. How long had he been running? A couple of weeks? Because I had watched him run after that night. He had gone so far away in such an infinitesimal amount of time that I had become convinced I was the plague.

"—Is there something else going on?" he pressed. "Why do you keep giving me mixed signals? One minute, we're happy and then we're ignoring each other." Liam sighed through his deep adolescent torment. "The nicest thing you could've done is throw it out in a hidden place. Fuck, at least I wouldn't have to deal with the 'she hates me' crap."

"I'm sorry Liam, but I'm being honest. I really did like it. I threw it out because I'm not much of a preserver." I was no fucking museum—did he expect me to be? Maybe he did. Maybe that explained why for much of our relationship, Liam had flaunted me in public as if I were an exhibit instead of a human being. "And you know what," I growled, leaning into him. "I do hate you. In fact, I despise you. I've been doing it since that day you left."

That was when he shamelessly and utterly baffled me by cornering me into a bookcase, pressing his body against mine. Despite my anger, my my heartbeat accelerated. Our noses grazed. His breath pooled onto mine. My lips brushed against his neck. My body erupted with undesirable tingles. I became fragmented once more.

"So this is innocent then," he said. "None of this means anything to you anymore."

It did though. And maybe it was the exuberance of human nature or the intimacy of the moment, but when I responded with silence, Liam had gotten his answer. He asserted his authority with a satisfied grin. That was the last thing I saw before he crashed his lips onto mine.

Chapter 18

LIAM'S lips were rough, like ashy cigarettes and year-old rain. I told myself that I couldn't enjoy this—that I wasn't enjoying it—and that more than anything, I was leading him on; I was just physically satisfying myself in the process. It was morbid, but my mind functioned in strange ways.

Liam released his hands from mine, where they had previously been intertwined, not breaking our kiss. It was then that he placed it on my chest—the area of heartbeat and vulnerability—and slowly trailed it down to my waist, where he momentarily rested, before gliding it behind to squeeze my buttocks. That was when I decided that physical submission was not worth it if it did not accompany emotional investment; I pushed him away.

"I'm sorry, I—I can't go there," I mumbled. A part of me worried that I had disappointed him.

His fingers caressed my cheek. My body had gotten accustomed to his effect. It seemed to dissipate with every additional moment I spent with him. There was no burn. Not like Molly had described. Electricity, she had claimed. That was the effect of Declan's touch. Why was I becoming indifferent to Liam—my first love? I wondered if Declan's words of conquests had value; now that I had won Liam over—now that I knew it—he no longer mattered to me.

Maybe it's because you're interested in his brother, idiot.

I slapped myself on the forehead. Screw me for getting sadistic thoughts. I quickly pushed Liam out of my way and grabbed my bag, giving him a hasty wave before rushing out of the library.

I walked slowly. It gave the time to think. However, after walking for a little while, I infamously bumped into someone. I looked up, straightening myself in the process. Who I saw startled me. How was it that we had developed this tendency to constantly bump into each other?

"Uh, sorry, I didn't mean to bump into you," I said lamely.

Declan chuckled. His laughter sounded like music to my ears. I chastised myself for wanting to be further serenaded. "It's fine. I'm used to thus. Us always crashing like this."

"Uh," I drawled, not knowing what to say. "I was just heading out."

"Can I join you?"

"No," I said, a bit too quickly. I slumped, releasing a sigh. "You probably don't want to. I know you have better things to do."

Declan smiled. "Not at all. I fancy a chat with the school's cynic."

I covered my face with my hands, resisting my embarrassment. "Be prepared to die of boredom," I warned him. "I'm feeling really out of it today." And it might have to do with the fact that I just kissed your brother.

His lips widened into a broader grin, the gesture meeting his eyes. Then we walked alongside one another. Even when we weren't touching, I felt something with him that I hadn't felt with Liam. Our hands were inches apart, dangling freely, and I fancied the idea of Declan and I falling in love—being liberated at last, together.

"Here we are," he sang once our feet stepped onto the concrete out of our campus. We occupied a nearby bench and indulged in silence until he broke it. "So? How are you?"

"I'm fine!" I chirped. "What's up with you?"

"Nothing much. Just hanging around."

"With Molly?"

Declan laughed at her mention. "Maybe."

I reciprocated the laugh despite sinking a little on the inside. When Declan gaped at me in return, I suppressed the laughter and plummeted into questions of insecurity. Had I laughed for too long? Did it sound bad? Was there something on my teeth?

"Avery, seriously? That was the most unconvincing laugh I had ever heard in my life."

I gasped, feigning hurt. "Are you telling me how I feel, Declan Andrews?"

"Maybe I am."

"I don't think you can," I murmured truthfully. How could he when I couldn't do it myself?

"Avery?" he said then.

I knew it. I knew that tone. That inquisitive, challenging tone. Declan was going to ask me about Liam again. He was going to ask me about that night.

"Yeah?"

"Have you ever felt guilty for liking somebody other than the one you're supposed to?"

I gulped. Did he know..? No, he couldn't.

"Uh, not exactly," I lied. "Why do you ask?"

"No, it's not—I mean—well, I've never felt it," he stuttered. "I—I, I was just wondering."

"That was an unconvincing statement," I deadpanned, unimpressed.

Declan ran his fingers through his hair. "How about a secret for a secret then? I'll tell you about me and you can tell me about Liam and you."

I nodded, holding out my pinky. "Pinky promise," I said.

Declan wrapped his pinky around mine, and in came the charge. "Pinky promise."

I yanked my finger away abruptly because with that simple touch, my heart had gathered inexplicable motion. I even wondered if he heard it beating.

"Her name was Anna," he started. "I shattered her world. Well, that's what she told me before she left. But when she left, she shattered my world and everything in it." He eyed me for permission before continuing. When I nodded my head, he cleared his throat, then biting softly into his lower lip continued speaking. "Okay, her name was Anna—"

"Yeah, you said that."

"So, her name is Anna..."

"Declan," I drawled, annoyance seeping in. I let him continue anyway.

"Anna—she believed in love. She thought Plato was right, that we were put on earth to find our other halves. She read Greek mythology and spoke of epic heroes falling in love with heroines. Then she met me.

"She was never strong. She relied on a lot of people. She had relied on me. And I betrayed her with that philosophy that I have of people being no more than conquests. I used her, tortured her for my own amusement, and when it was all over, when the day came that she left, I realized that the stories she would read of love had come from a place of truth."

I placed my hand on his cold ones to comfort him. Though startled, he continued, "I was unable to forget her. First loves, yeah? It became harder after her. No one I met could compare. No one has. But I'm the bastard—I used her."

"Declan?" I spoke his name softly, feeling remorseful for interrupting him.

"Mm?"

"You aren't—a bastard. Dickhead, yes. Messed up in the head, definitely. But you're also sweet. You're an mysterious and intriguing. Don't blame yourself for what happened with Anna. It happens. Love is circumstantial, after all."

"I don't like Molly the way she wants me to," he blurted out. With that confession and the grimace that overtook his face, I could see the way this tortured him: his inability to commit to people. "I just—I get bored. Others bore me."

All I could wish was that I was not boring him and that I was even a fragment of what Anna was to him. Declan was in love with her. Could he ever feel that way about me?

"You should talk to her," I encouraged. "Don't play with her too, Declan. Especially after that whole promise ring fiasco you pulled."

He nodded. "I know. It's just—hard."

"Why did you start this anti-love crusade of yours, anyway?"

"Because rejection hurts," he admitted sheepishly. "It's hard to reject others at first."

I nodded, somehow understanding. And even though I could not fully empathize with him, the realization that he was not as apathetic as he let on comforted me.

"Now," he digressed. "You need to tell me about Liam."

I froze, my face falling.

"You promised, Avery!"

I considered it before realizing that it was too painful. "I—I can't."

"Please," he pleaded, his eyes glistening with hope. "I want to know you, Ave."

"Fine," I mumbled, caving into his gaze. "I'll tell you."

He smirked victoriously.

"But you won't tell anyone, okay?"

He gave me a thumbs up and provided an assuring smile. I weakly returned the gesture. "Well, Liam and I—where do I begin? We met when we were ten, during that age when boys were creatures of the dark and held cooties. Somehow, we became close. As years passed and we matured, one day he asked me to go on a date with him.

"It was surreal, being with him. He made the idea of soulmates seem not so far-fetched. Then came the rumors a year later: everyone saying Liam had begun sleeping around. I trusted him completely; I always had. Then I caught him with somebody, Declan. Liam. The love of my life. My future. This guy that I thought I would marry. Tangled with somebody else." I bit my lip to suppress my tears. "It was hard," I explained, my voice cracking. A gentle tear trickled down my cheeks. It was hot and prickly, the way Liam's lips had felt. "I left the room in a blur because I was too upset to even see who it was under the covers.

"I blamed myself for it. I thought he was my fucking soulmate," I hesitated as I said these words, "and he just tore me apart. When you're in those youthful years and in love, nothing matters but those feelings. There is no social order. Nothing political. Just an innocent sense of love. When we ended, we did too quickly and

Liam left my life that very week and I am just seeing him now."

He began offering words of comfort, but they only intensified my desire to cry. "I should go," I muttered, hating that Declan was seeing me like this: so week and vulnerable, an easy prey.

"Yeah, I should go too," he said, but his eyes told a different story. Stay, they seemed to say.

He remained glued to his seat even as I got up, as if he was latching onto the remnants of his beautiful moment. Without another word, I grabbed my bag and headed in the direction of my dorm room. If it felt spacious any other day, it was closing in on me today.

But I would be lying if I said a weight had not been lifted over my shoulders. I trusted that Declan would preserve my secret—that he would help me overcome it—because we were friends now, officially; and that is how all stories begin, don't they?

CHAPTER 19

"WHERE were you yesterday?"

"Nowhere."

"Why weren't you answering my calls?"

"I don't know. I was busy."

"Oh my god! Why wasn't Declan answering my calls?"

I sighed, eyeing Molly as she widened her eyes dramatically. I almost felt bad for her. Her infatuation had transformed into an obsession. With more time Declan spent away from her—which he was doing increasingly more of—the more insane she became.

We were in the cafeteria, eating lunch.

Molly twirled her hair around her finger, her eyes not leaving mine. "I called him a couple of times yesterday. Called you too, Avery. No answers. Nada. No text replies, either."

I ate in silence.

"...Ho-lee cow!" she shrieked ."Could he be cheating on me?"

"Molly," I snapped, rolling my eyes. "Stop this drama. You're better than this."

"I know you were with him," she deadpanned, her jealousy radiating off her as ultraviolet waves do from the sun. Her aura was vengeful, laced with a toxic undertone. "And what do you know about anything, Avery? Just because you're his chemistry partner you think you know him."

"Art, partner," I mumbled, correcting her.

Molly and I bickered back and forth. She was bright red with anger and embarrassment by the end of our transaction and Joey—poor Joey—was caught in the middle, helplessly acting as a mediator between the two of us.

"Avery. I know this is sudden," Molly began, "but do you like my boyfriend?"

I choked on my food, coughing violently for a moment's worth before glancing at her. "What the fuck? Like, for the record, we're talking about Declan here, right?"

"I've been studying you lately," she murmured. "You seem into him."

"Well, no, I am not into him," I replied nervously. Every bone in my body shivered with unease. "Actually, I think I'm getting feelings for Liam again," I lied innocuously.

"Good," Molly asserted. All she wanted was to affirm her territorial claim on Declan. "Liam deserves you and you deserve him."

At that, I bit my tongue to suppress unleashing a string of angry words. I deserved more than Liam. How could she even suggest that knowing what I had been through with him? Liam and I didn't deserve each other—not in the faintest.

"Speak of the devil," Joey muttered, motioning behind me.

"Hey guys," a familiar voice said. It was Liam. "Mind if Razor and I grab a seat here?"

"Sure," Molly mumbled with a dismissive flick of her wrist. Her mind was clearly elsewhere. Of course not for long—Razor and Liam managed to get giggles from her. Her mind was eventually diverted from Declan, the origin of conflict, and she was a free spirit again. As the four—Razor, Joey, Molly and Liam—began immersing in a conversation about something I cared very little about, I got up and left.

The hallways were vacant. I led myself to the exit. When I left the building, I found myself encountering the girls—Valarie and Allen—from months ago. The day I had met Declan. The day everything changed. That very day when a chapter of my life ended and another began without my knowing. I wondered if today was another one of those important days in hindsight.

The winds were crisp, but the warmth of the incoming spring prevailed. I seated myself beside a fountain and began caressing the water, counting the pennies that had been dropped within.

"Wilson?"

I continued stroking the water, letting its coldness send shivers down my spine.

"Wilson?"

I raised my head, turning it around. "What do you want, Andrews?"

"Why sitting alone?"

"No specific reason," I answered with a shrug.

Unconvinced, Declan occupied the seat next to me. "You sure."

"Estoy seguro," I told him in the little Spanish that I knew.

"Declaring your undying love for me in a different language?" he jested.

I hate that I like you so much, I thought. I said nothing. "Sod off," I told him eventually.

He leaned in and rubbed my chin with the tip of his thumb: a brave move. "Touch me again and I'll—I'll punch you," I threatened. If he did, I may disintegrate.

He chuckled, accepting the challenge by exploring my face: beginning with the birthmark beside my eyes to my cheeks, and then my lips, and then me jaw—I shoved his hands away. "Stop this, Declan."

"So, you were saying?" he taunted. "You're going to punch my face in?"

"I would, but I don't want to see you hurt," I retorted.

Declan smirked. "Try me."

So I did—I punched him as hard as I could on his chest. A jarring impact. Declan didn't wince. He didn't even budge. He was enjoying this, taking pride in my embarrassment.

"Avery, what the hell was that?"

"A punch."

He chuckled fleetingly. "Somebody needs to teach you how to throw a good punch."

"Are you volunteering?"

"Maybe I am."

"So teach me," I told him. "Teach me to throw a good punch, Andrews. It'll come to good use when I can finally use it on you."

He laughed once again. Then silence overcame us.

"Hey Avery?" he said at last, his fingers toying with the edge of my dress.

I looked up. "Yeah?"

"I think I'm starting to like you," he confessed haphazardly.

Taken aback, I gawked at him, wondering if I had heard him right. "What?"

"I like you," he repeated. "And in a way I'm not supposed to."

I forgot how to breathe.

CHAPTER 20

"WHAT?"

That was, of course, my genius answer. What do you do when a guy confesses his feelings for you? You repeat the word 'What?' until he begins to question his decision.

"I said—"

I pressed my lips together. "I know what you said."

Declan was squeamish. If he wanted to say anything more, he suppressed the urge effortlessly. I wondered what Molly would say if she knew that this was what her alleged boyfriend was up to.

"Declan," I said exasperatedly. I floundered for words, unsure of what to say. Was it okay to cave in to my senses and kiss him until our insides numbed? Or did that kind of stuff only happen in romance novels? "You're dating my best friend, for fuck's sake," I said once clarity seeped on.

He evaded my accusations as if they did not faze him. "I only did it to get under your skin," he defended. "And it's clearly working because I know you feel the same way about me. The conversations we have—just us. We're unique, Ave."

I released a weary sigh. "I can't do this."

"You agree though," he began hesitantly. "You feel the same way about me?"

"Maybe," I said in a quiet, regretful voice. "Maybe just like one percent."

It was then that Declan began to laugh. Taken aback, I examined his movements, the way his eyes glistened in mirth as his lips released a sound personifying his shock and amusement. "Avery," he released in between fits of uncontrollable laughter. "I was only joking!"

I stared at him as he laughed—gaped. How could I have forgotten about his insensitivity?

"You know I don't believe in love, Avery," he told me, reaffirming his cynical stance. And I was allegedly the cynic. Declan's pessimism for love was beyond what I held; I was bitter about a failed relationship. For him, it sounded like something more.

And I then felt cold.

"So you like me," he reaffirmed once his laughter died down

"No," I replied quickly. A bit too quickly. "I was just playing along."

Though unconvinced, he said, "Good. Don't fall in love with me, okay?"

I nodded my head in assurance as if that was something I could help. As if love was voluntary. As if we chose to love those who would never love us in return. As if we chose the heartache and emotional torment. With these thoughts in mind, I looked at him in dismay, hoping that the intensity of my gaze made him realize how bizarre he sounded. I played along anyway.

"I promise to never fall in love with you," I mumbled, crossing my fingers for having lied.

"You better not."

"I won't."

"Good."

"Avery? Avery Wilson?" emerged a voice from the loud speaker, interrupting our motions. "Please report to the main office. Avery Wilson."

"That's my cue to leave," I said when the voice died off.

He nodded. "So maybe it is."

"Come with me?" I pleaded. He was in his humanitarian mood, I suppose, because he obediently trailed behind me on our journey to the main office. When there, the secretary told me that I had a call waiting for me in the phone room. Giving Declan a wave of momentary farewell, I found myself inside with a phone to my ears. "Hello?"

"Avery!" Mom's voice emerged from the other end of the line. My face fell. "How are you dear?"

"Mom," I sneered. "I'm fine, thank you. How are you?"

"I'm good," she replied, a frown conspicuously on her face given her jaded tone.

"Ave," she started softly. She let a momentary silence linger. "Please start packing. You have to come here for Christmas. No compromises. We'll come and pick you up early next Friday, okay?"

"Mom," I snapped. "I have plans."

"What? Who could you have possible made plans with?"

"I'm going with dad," I lied. I had more bitter visions for Christmas: sitting before a fireplace bawling my eyes out because I was so undeniably and utterly lonely.

"About your dad..."

My eyes widened. "What about dad?"

"Sweetie, he's not leaving rehab anytime soon. If anything, he is struggling more than ever—"

"You're lying," I interjected brashly, my voice rising in octaves due to anger. "You're just saying this to make me come with you. I won't. I'm not going with you."

"Avery—"

I ignored my mom's pleas, pressing the end call button on the phone. I sighed after I did, questioning my decision and discerning the phone intimately. Why did I have to have such a dysfunctional family? Why was it that speaking to my mother made me see the worst in existence? She was not spiteful—she hadn't been in a while—but the agonies of the past accumulated in such a way that you blinded yourself to the beauty of the present.

A finger gently tapped my back and I turned around. It was then that I realized I had been crying—again. Twice this week. What was happening to me?

Before I could shed any more tears, I ran. I ran out of that room—out of that hallway. Concerned footsteps pounded behind me. It was Declan, of course; he was the last person I wanted to see.

I shrugged off the polarity in my emotions as I stopped at the end of the vacant hallway, sitting down with my chest convulsing in a paroxysm of chokes and sobs. I was crying so viciously and it was difficult to understand why. I wanted to revert to the past: to the days of Mom and I, when we had our relationship intact, and of Liam and I. Nostalgia was the end.

Before I could atone it, Declan had slipped beside me and his arms were snaking around my waist, forming a sanctuary at their wake. So immersed in the moment, I cried into his arms for everything that had been lost.

"Why do you have to be so fucking nice?" I asked him in the in-betweens. "Why the fuck are you always being so nice to me?"

"Avery," he murmured, soothing my back. "It's okay. This is what friends are for, right?"

"Right," I muttered in distaste. "Friendship. Yeah."

"Come on, stop crying," he pleaded. "Please? It feels weird. You used to be so headstrong. What the fuck happened to you?"

I closed my eyes, resisting a sigh. "You," I whispered. "You're what happened."

Declan loosened our embrace, staring at me quietly but intimately. "What do you mean?"

"I'm sorry," I apologized, brushing him off. "I'm sorry that I'm emotional like this."

"What are you going on about?"

"It's just—I like you!" I released at last. With that confession, the burden of my feelings were lifted from on my shoulders. I was an unfaithful friend to Molly, I realized then, and I despised myself for having gotten so immersed in the intimacy of the moment. I hated that I was vulnerable. I hated that Declan was here through it all.

He leaned against the wall, folding his arms across his chest. "When did this happen?"

"I don't know."

"How did this happen?"

"It—It just did."

"Why did you promise to never fall in love with me, then?"

"I don't love you yet."

He sighed, coursing his fingers through his hair. After a silence that followed, he said, "Avery, this love shit. It doesn't fucking exist, okay?"

"It happened between you and Anna," I pointed out.

"It was unrequited," he shot defensively.

"It still happened though."

"Love only happens in romance novels," he deadpanned, and it stung. It stung like shrapnel colliding on naked skin, like stubborn fire caressing the tips of your fingers against your will.

"So maybe it does," I managed to choke out. "But I don't fucking love you yet, Declan, okay?"

He looked tense, a mixture of confusion, anger, and regret crossing his face with equivocal volatility. Before he could say anything else, I stormed out of there. I regretted everything too. I regretted the day I met him. I regretted the day I started talking to him. And most of all, I regretted the day I had started feeling even a trickle of attraction toward him.

CHAPTER 21

AVOIDING Declan wasn't the easiest thing to do, but I managed it in the days that followed. It was Wednesday morning and I was in my dorm room, wrapped under a cocoon of blankets. I was dejectedly considering the fact that our art assignment was due in presentation in a few days.

I lay on bed, staring at the dull white ceiling. I was in no mood to go to class, so I decided to ditch for the day. Christmas being next week, Molly had told me that she was leaving today.

After a few more minutes in bed, I rolled over for some more, indulging in Netflix. The morn-

ing uneventfully passed by with my fantasiz-
ing over The Arrow—Olicity for days—and then
The Flash—West-Allen for days—and then me
preparing a gift for Molly. I had bought it during
the monotonous days that followed: a photo
frame. In it was a photo of Molly and I: my arms
around her shoulders with passionate grins on
our faces.

Memories never fade was inscribed on the
frame.

I placed the frame atop my nightstand, freezing in the next moment when I heard a giggling
sound. My eyes darted towards the door. It was
precisely then that I saw the back of Molly's
head—her dangling blonde curls—and Liam; he
pressed her against the wall in a gesture of
intimacy. My jaw dropped open and I stared at
the two of them in utter confusion.

Upon seeing me, Liam pushed her away.

"Babe," Molly said. "What's wrong?"

When Liam answered with silence, Molly
turned on her heel to where his eyes were: on

me. Then she disintegrated. "Avery," she gasped. "Shouldn't you be in class?"

"I don't know," I snapped, glowering at her. The extremity of the situation had yet to sink in. "Shouldn't you?"

"I decided to take the day off. And I just happened to crash into Liam, so—"

Then it hit me.

"You were the one," I stated, recognition seeping in. "You were the girl Liam left me for all those years ago."

Molly gulped, guilty as charged. It was in her silence that I found my answer. Then I wondered how I had missed it. So it was her, I thought, wondering why. How? How was it that the girl who had stolen my first love from me was no other than my best friend?

I glanced at her face that had slackened with remorse, but she was just remorseful for having gotten caught. If she hadn't, she would continue this. Liam would continue this. "And you," I told him, suppressing the tears that seeped into my face. "What was that bit about people deserving second chances, Liam? You're a dickhead."

"Avery, we—" Molly began.

I grabbed the friendship frame from my nightstand and shoved it onto Molly's chest. She caught it with an uneasy gulp. "You know what, Molly," I said in the calmest voice I could conjure. "Memories never fade. And this one never fucking will." With that, I grabbed my sweater and bolted—away from there, from Molly and Liam, and from what I knew of my life then.

I wound up in the school's junkyard with my back pressed against a brick wall. I stared at the sky, shouting, "I'm the unluckiest girl in the world!" The screaming helped. Unfortunately it was not enough. "I don't want to go with home," I blubbered incoherently. "I don't want to go—"

A familiar voice spoke up from the distance, garnering my attention. "You said the same thing last year, Avery," she said—Joey.

"I know," I replied. "I don't want to go. But I don't want to be here either. So where do I go?"

"Anywhere you want, love," she said. "The world is in our fingertips."

"That's a myth," I retorted mindlessly.

"Not quite."

"I'm not in a position to ask Mom for a loan," I told her. When Joey faltered, I added, "I'm sorry. I just saw Molly with Liam—just awful images still stuck in my mind of the two of them together."

She raised an eyebrow, walking closer toward me. "Molly and Liam? Seriously?

I nodded.

"So it was her all along," she speculated, placing the pieces together effortlessly.

"Seems so."

"So now your crush on Declan doesn't seem so bad," she said, the corners of her lips twitching into a smile. "It seems reasonable, love. And maybe that explains this," she concluded, reaching into her pockets for a paper that she eventually dropped onto my palm.

"What is it?" I asked.

"I'm not entirely sure," she explained sheep-ishly. "It's just—Declan told me to give it to you. And he was urgent about it so open it."

I did.

"What does it say?" Joey pressed.

I bit my lip in contemplation, staring down at the piece of paper. "That he wants to meet me." Then I glanced at Joey. "Is this a sign?"

She released a fleeting laugh. "Are you looking for a sign?"

I nodded.

In fact I was.

CHAPTER 22

MAYBE I walked. Maybe I ran. At any rate, he was there before I was: standing before the entrance where we had met for the first time. My first bumping into him: it was supposed to be a chance encounter that allotted to nothing but it had an adverse affect, didn't it? It had been the beginning of everything that amounted to he and I.

"Avery," he said as soon as he saw me, a resolve clear in his eyes. "You wanted to talk to me?"

I raised an eyebrow in confusion. "What? You were the one who told me to come here."

He let his confusion show through his furrowed eyebrows. I examined him then: his messy hair, disheveled from having run his fingers through it so many times, and his eyes of ice as rumors had advertised; they were never far off. When my eyes wandered to his lips, I resisted an urge to press him unto a wall and kiss him senseless.

"Joey," he began to explain, revealing a white sheet of paper. "She said—"

I lifted a similar paper of my own, the one allegedly from Declan. "Joey," I realized. Then came the realization that Declan hadn't wanted to see me; it was all a ploy by Joey. Knowing that it was too brutal—that I could hardly reconcile with any of this—I swiveled on my heel to leave for good. As I escaped, a soft, troubled groan escaped Declan's lips. With a newfound resolve, he grabbed my waist, spinning me around before I could get far. "Declan," I began to say. My eyes widened as he pressed his body against mine, pinning me against a nearby wall.

"Enough," he demanded. "Enough of this."

I was at a loss for words.

"I'm sorry, okay?" he continued. "I'm sorry that I'm a dick who keeps running in loops. I'm sorry that I realize how important people are to me only when they're convinced that I'm an ass-hole."

"Declan," I began.

He shook his head. "No, Avery, please. Just this past week has been absolute torture without you in it. And it's crazy because we're not in love—we're kids. But I'm into you. I want more of you," he hammered home. He was impossible to resist in that moment. My shameless mind envisioned this passion manifesting as wild, in-tangible motions that set sheets on fire.

"Molly and I are over too," he continued. "So we don't have to worry about that. We don't have to worry about anything anymore."

"Just one thing," I murmured.

He glanced at me curiously.

"Kind of worried that you might get me a promise ring too," I jested.

His lips morphed into a grin. Without another word nor insinuation, he pressed his lips unto mine. His was a flavor of longing and affection. It was milk chocolate and the late summer rains. It was bliss in an action if such a thing existed, and you decoded the cause of my happiness to its most inane state, it would be in the person I saw myself become in that moment when him.

There was no synchronicity. There was no electricity. There was acceptance—a sense of familiarity—and an optimism for what would come. When we pulled away at last, we were breathless but ecstatic. We were kids. We were naive. Yet that naivety was all that we had.

CHAPTER 23

DECLAN was not Van Gogh, but he came close. He had painted a piece messing with the motif of clocks, about love being a product of circumstance. "Love happens in these moments," he explained to our art class during our presentation. "It is not constant. It changes. It is fluid. But commitment—" He took a deep breath. "—frankly, it's one of the bravest thing in the word. It means you're taking a risk with this person who may very much chance, but relying that their love for you will not anyway."

I glanced at him in awe. As did Mr. Camia. Then when it was my turn to speak, I talked about how much I had grown in this art project. "I thought about doing it on how love makes us irrational and wrongly exuberant. Then things happened. Then more things." I resisted a smile, stealing a coy glance at Declan. "And now I believe that it is something worth experiencing and preserving."

Mr. Camia smiled proudly at us. "Amazing job, guys. Truly two stellar and completing pieces. They are clearly so different and yet can come together in so many ways. What a great way to end the unit and start winter break, Avery and Declan."

I nodded in acknowledgement and felt my heart gathering warmth. We did a question and answer session and the class applauded to signal the end of our presentation. Once in the back of the room, Declan chuckled airily, his lips stealing a touch at the nape of my neck.

I disintegrated all at once.

I loaded my suitcase on the trunk of Mark's car. For once in her life, Mom had remained true to her words. She had arrived to take me away for

Christmas. A grand escape, she promised, but I was devastated to be away from Declan.

"So, Avery, how is school coming along?" Mark questioned—small-talk, I supposed.

"It's fine," I responded curtly.

"Sounds good—oh," Mark exclaimed, motioning behind me. "You have some visitors."

I turned around to see Declan and Joey coming in this direction. I closed the hood and gave them a little wave. "Hey guys," I said once they were close enough.

"You hoe," Joey chastised. "Why didn't I knew you were leaving until this boy—" She motioned dramatically toward Declan. "—told me?"

I laughed and pulled her into an embrace. "I'll miss you, love," she said as we pulled away. She then took out a starling box from her pocket and handed it over. "Merry Christmas."

I reached into my pocket for a box of my own. "Merry Christmas, my love," I told her.

"Okay then, I'll leave you two to it," she said, referring to Declan and I. "Bye Avery!"

As Joey left, Declan enclosed the proximity between us. He tucked a strand of hair behind my ear. "I wish I would spend the holidays with you," he said dejectedly.

"I wish it too," I murmured longingly. "But we'll see each other in—two weeks?"

"I want to kiss you right now," he admitted, scratching the back of his ear. "Can I?"

"Do you have to ask?" I chastised, rolling my eyes.

He inched closer to me, his lips grazing mine.

"Avery!" a familiar feminine voice piped in: Mom. "I have all your paperwork. It's time to go."

I closed my eyes, pressing my lips into Declan's. "You take care of yourself, loser," I told him. "Fuck," I cursed then. "I already miss you, you idiot."

He placed his forehead on mine, gazing in a downward motion at me. "I'll miss you more."

"Avery! It's time to go. Get in the car," Mom shouted.

I wanted to yell at her to just shut the fuck up. Instead, I kissed Declan again. And again. And again. "Bye Declan," I told him with a tone of finality.

He provided a weak smile. With a final kiss, I left him. In the car, Mom had the aura of a newspaper reporter, her eyes attentive. "Avery, was that your boyfriend?" she asked interrogatively.

I absentmindedly nodded my head. "I know, mom," I muttered tentatively. "I'm not allowed to have a boyfriend. But he's—"

"He's decent," she finished. "You're young. In love. I get it."

Mark began to drive. We engaged in meaningless chatter until we managed to make it to the highway. The sunset grazed the distant horizon, a myriad of reds and pinks and blues glittering the late spring skies. With my eyes surrounded by beauty and by heart beating for a certain boy that embodied it, I fell into a long, placid sleep.

"Avery? Wake up."

I groaned, pushing my hands into my earlobes. "Avery, we're home. Wake up"

My eyelids slowly fluttered open. I yawned drowsily and rubbed my eyes. The first thing I saw was Mom. Not the best image to be woken up by. "Home?" I questioned. I had thought her arrival at my school and my departure from Declan was a nightmare. Instead, I had woken into a nightmare.

"Yeah, come on, get up and I'll take you to your room," she said.

"Okay," I mumbled, getting out of the car.

The crickets chirped as I entered Mom's two-story house. A crepuscule was in full motion. The color of her glorious above was white—a peaceful choice—with beige-colored steel roofs. She helped me dispatch my luggage and led me to my room, leaving me there for the night.

After adjusting myself, I decided to call Declan to let him know that I had arrived at home. After seven rings—yes I counted—someone picked up at last. "Hello?"

"Declan!" I beamed. "I'm home"

"This isn't—Declan," the voice said dejectedly.

My eyes widened. "Liam?"

"No," the person responded. "This is Declan's father. Can I please know who this is?"

"This is Avery," I replied politely. "I'm a good friend of Declan's. Can you please give him the phone?"

There was a pause in the other end.

"Declan is in the hospital," his father started. "Him and Liam got in a car accident earlier today. Both of them are severely injured and under ICU care."

A startled gasp escaped my lips. "Is this a joke?" I asked, disappointingly unamused. "Declan, tell me it's you. Tell me you're only joking with me.

"This isn't a joke," the receiver answered. "Can I please know where this call is from?"

I dropped my phone on the bed and broke into sobs. No...it couldn't be.

CHAPTER 24

DECLAN was in the hospital. Declan was in the hospital. Declan was in the hospital. Declan was in the hospital. Declan was in the hospital. Declan was in the hospital. Declan was in the hospital. Declan was in the hospital. Declan was in the hospital. Declan was in the hospital. Declan was in the hospital. Declan was in the hospital. I was a disintegrating mess of sobs and helplessness. For minutes on end, I had simply cried. What else was I to do?

"Avery? Dinner is—wait, honey, what's wrong?" Mom asked, barging into the room.

"Mom," I managed to choke out, however hoarse. "It's Declan, my boyfriend—my friend. He got into an accident or something like that. He's hurt. Mom, he's—" I curled into a ball, buying my head in my hands and releasing my devastation through a paroxysm of uncontrollable choking and sobbing. Mom rubbed my back in the limited consolation she could offer.

"We can go to the hospital," she said. "Where are they? Do you know?"

I didn't respond. How could I? I didn't know. I hadn't even bothered asking. I quickly wiped my eyes with my sweater sleeves and picked up my phone from the floor. Dialing Declan's number once more, I was relieved when Mr. Andrews answered the phone. Unable to speak, I forced the cellphone onto my mom.

"Avery? Is everything oka—oh," Mark exclaimed, stopping when he saw me. He glanced at my mother through his confusion and concern. Mom was listening intently to what the receiver was saying—Mr. Andrews giving her directions, I assumed.

"Yes," I finally heard her say. "We can come—No, no, it's no trouble—I understand, is everything fine now?—In which hospital is he in? Okay. Good bye. Take care." Once the call had ended, Mom addressed me as if I were a fragile china, only to be reckoned with in extreme caution. "Avery," she murmured. "They're in a hospital two hours away in the inner city. Have some dinner and sleep and tomorrow—"

"No," I interjected firmly. "I have to go today. Now. He could die, mom!"

She let a potential argument dwindle, caving in. "Okay, okay. Mark, go start the car please."

And he did. But Mom drove. The entire journey felt like one into the catastrophic unknown.

CHAPTER 25

"HE'S in a coma, caused by trauma to the head when the car crash."

"We don't know when he'll wake up."

"We're not sure if he'll live."

"I'm very sorry..."

Declan lay on a bed of white, machines beeping around him, his chest rising and falling with peaceful steadiness. He looked as attractive as he was the first time I met him, and perhaps more handsome with his eyes closed as if he were simply taking a nap. Taking the seat beside the bed, I brushed his hair away from his forehead and as I did so, a drop of water spilled onto his cheek from the tears running from my eyes.

I had forced Mom to drive like a maniac to get to here as fast as possible hoping that the sooner I got here, the sooner good news would be on the way...

My hopes plummeted when I saw his figure.

"Declan," I whispered. "Wake up. Wake up, you asshole."

I could still hear the machines beeping un-steadily, but no matter how loud the machines were, Declan lay there, motionless.

"You know, I never thought this would hap-pen."

At this point, I was too perplexed by my own worry to make note of the fact that I was inco-herently speaking to an unconscious person.

"Remember when we first met? We hated each other. I hated your brother, but I kind of sort of loved him at the same time. Then somehow, through this big twisting shit of a mess, I began feeling this way about you..."

Another tear drop fell down my cheek.

"How could this happen?" I asked to no one in particular. "Besides the fact that you acted like a jerk when we first met, and you were still jerk when we became somewhat friends..." I laughed through my tears, quietly. "You need to wake up. Understand? I like you. A lot. So wake up. If you don't wake up...I'll...I'll kill you!"

The last part was meant to be a joke, but I couldn't help it. I burst into sobs so loud and heavy that I could hardly believe that it was me crying.

"Don't die on me! Don't, you stupid idiot!"

Grabbing his limp hand, I laced my fingers through his and squeezed tightly, enjoying the warmth. Even though Declan didn't budge, I felt myself heating up. He still had that effect on me, and he wasn't even conscious.

"I don't care how long you're going to be like this," I told him. "I'm going to wait for you. Got that? Take as long as you need. I'll always wait for you, Declan."

Moving forward, I placed a soft kiss against his unresponsive lips.

"I always will."

Epilogue

Two Years Later

Declan Andrews

I wake up from the strangest dream.

It's weird, because it wasn't really a dream. It was really a repeat of all my memories, starting from day one. Running along the beach with Liam when I was four. Wrestling with our dog, Timber, when I was five, and the sad day when he moved onto heaven when I was six. Having my first crush when I was seven—all those years finally coming back to me.

I slowly try to pry open my eyes but find that it is hard to. Either my eyes are closed, or it's too dark. Then I realize that it's not too dark; in fact, it's too bright. The light blinds my eyes as if they haven't opened in years. The room I'm in is entirely white.

"Am I dead?" I try to mutter. Instead, a pathetic croak comes out. Maybe this is what heaven looks like? All white and empty and so bright that it's blinding?

Suddenly, a loud beeping fills my ears. It completely disturbs me and causes a tepid headache. I wince, when suddenly; the door flies open when people come in. I don't recognize these people at all, and they're all wearing scrubs.

"He's awake!" I hear. "He's awake! He's awake!"

"Damn right I'm awake," I mutter under my breath.

Oh, good. My voice is working somewhat correctly, although it's kind of hoarse. What's with these people? It's not like I've been dead for three days and rose up again like Jesus or something. A middle aged man with glasses comes in among all the frenzy as people poke and prod me, asking me questions that make me crave for a hundred years in solitude—with Avery.

Where was Avery?

"Excuse me, can you tell me your name?" the man asks.

Deciding that there must be a reason for him asking, I answer, "Uh, yeah. Declan Andrews?"

"Good. Declan, where do you live?"

"In New York."

"Can you tell me your father's name?"

"Dexter Andrews."

"Your mother's name?"

"Lannie Andrews."

"How old are you, Declan?"

"I'm seventeen."

The man purses his lips like I got the question wrong. How could I? I scowl. I know how old I am.

"Declan, when's your birthday?"

"January 4th, 1994."

"I see..."

Irritated, I finally burst. "What's going on here?" I wince at the strain my vocal chords feel, as if they haven't been used in ages. "Why are you giving me that look? What am I doing here?"

"Do you really not remember?"

"Is there anything to remember?"

"Think, Declan." The gray eyes of the man pierce mine. "Think hard."

I lean back, growing a little woozy from sitting up straight for so long. It's when I do that that I realize how stiff my body is. And just like that, I'm thrown into a memory: the screech of breaks and untamed tires squealing along the road. An impact so jarring that I feel like my teeth are about to pop out. Glass shattering and the dizziness of being tossed round and round. Red liquid oozing into my eye, and next thing I know, sheer darkness following.

"No," I say quietly, and then moan. "No. Shit, no. How long have I been out? It couldn't have been that long. Right? No way..."

"Perhaps we should speak in a little bit..."

"No. Look, doctor, I don't know what your name is, but I seriously need you to tell me this. Just one thing, okay? I don't know anything else that's going on. So please, tell me. What's today's date?"

The doctor hesitates but eventually gives into the pleading look on my face. "April 14th—" I relax until he finishes. "—2014."

"What?!" I whisper-shout. To say that I am shocked is an understatement. There is no way over a year—a whole fucking year—has passed. "You mean..."

"You've been in coma since the December of 2012. It's a miracle that you're alive."

I can't think of anything to say.

"We're going to phone your parents. They'll come immediately."

"Wait, doctor!" I stop him just as he is about to leave, a realization finally dawning upon me. It has been over a year since I was last awake. Over a year since I have spoken to anybody. "Do you mind if I request that you call someone to get them here as soon as possible?"

"Of course not. Who do you have in mind?"

And so I tell him.

Seeing my parents cry from joy like that make tears fall too. I hug them close. When it comes time to hug Liam—whom I learned got out of the accident with only a broken bone and cracked collarbone—I don't even hesitate.

Everyone is happy. Everyone is smiling and crying and I notice how, over the past year, my family has aged. Dad has gray streaks in his hair and Mom is growing wrinkles that make her look more wiser by the second. Liam has grown too, his features accentuating since the last time I saw him, and he looks bigger—stronger.

It takes me a while to accept that a year of my life is gone. Just like that, I am nineteen.

"Are you sure you're okay?" Mom asks feverishly. "No headaches? Chest pains? Nothing?"

"Nothing at all, Mom. I promise, I'm fine. Just ...please, relax a bit."

"Honey, you've been in coma for nearly two years! It's hard to relax," she exclaims. Beside the anxiety in her voice, she smiles.

"You're certainly a tough one," Dad says. "There were times when the doctors told us that there was no way, but you're here."

Whatever Dad says is drowned out by a soft tap on the door. It swings open and, because of the crowd of family members around me, all I see are red heels.

"Excuse me?" a familiar voice says politely. "Can I speak to Declan?"

"Oh, of course. Come on, Dexter, Liam. Let's give the two a little privacy." Mom ushers Dad and Liam out of the hospital room against their protests. The door slams shut behind them.

I look up and gaze at her face: dark hair tumbling down, longer than I remember. Large, intelligent eyes, sparkling and filled with immense joy and tears that trickle down her cheeks. She looks—beautiful. "Avery."

"Declan," she says.

"Hi," I finish lamely, and she laughs.

"Hi," Avery, my girlfriend—was she ever mine?—whispers back.

I guess she is still my girlfriend, because the first thing she does is whip her head back towards the door. "Hey, what are you doing—" I begin to say but I am interrupted by her rapid movements. Before I can think, she leans down and presses her lips—hard—against mine. Though it has been nearly two years, my muscles react and I reach up to grab her neck and pull her closer to me. The feel of her soft mouth against mine...how could I have gone so long without it? "Avery," I say with awe.

"Hush," she says. She sits on the bed, wrapping herself around me. "You're still recovering, I guess. But it's okay now, right?" Holding me tighter she says, "I've been in fucking hell for the past two years."

All I can tell her is that I am sorry.

"Yeah, asshole," she snaps. "Be sorry! How the hell could you just leave me like that?"

"I just—"

She hushes me again. "Just, please. Whatever you do, don't leave me again, okay?"

I pull back and, dismissing the fact that I am still recovering and that I have lost a year from my life, I kiss her with the darkest passion I can conjure. It is my form of assurance. The kisses taste sour and sweet all at the same time, entwining all that has been lost with all that we have left, and I focus on nothing but the friction between us. The sense of belonging that we share in that moment, I realize, is all we need, then and forever.

It is all anyone needs.